I0645755

CORPORATE CHRISTMAS

BERNADETTE MARIE

5 Prince Publishing

Published by 5 PRINCE PUBLISHING & BOOKS, LLC

PO Box 865, Arvada, CO 80001

www.5PrinceBooks.com

ISBN digital: 978-1-63112-239-2

ISBN print: 978-1-63112-441-9

Custom cover by Marianne Nowicki at
www.PremadeEbookCoverShop.com

To Stan,
Merry Christmas
Love, Your Boss

ACKNOWLEDGMENTS

To my beautiful boys: As much as I miss Santa, I love working with you.

To my mommy and sissy: I cherish our many, many partnerships.

To my daddy: Thank you for my work ethic.

To Cate: Thank you for working with me and making me look flawless.

To my readers: Thank you for keeping me in business. I love what I do.

Thank you to Walt Disney for creating my favorite place to NOT work.

Encore

Finding Hope

THE THREE MRS. MONROES TRILOGY

Amelia

Penelope

Vivian

THE ASPEN CREEK SERIES

First Kiss

Unexpected Admirer

On Thin Ice

Indomitable Spirit

THE DENVER BRIDE SERIES

Cart Before the Horse

Never Saw it Coming

Candy Kisses

ROMANTIC SUSPENSE

Chasing Shadows

PARANORMAL ROMANCES

The Tea Shop

The Last Goodbye

HOLIDAY FAVORITES

Corporate Christmas

CORPORATE CHRISTMAS

Bernadette Marie

CHAPTER 1

*B*ells. They rang on high and they rang in the doorway of the buildings across the street—and they never stopped until Christmas had come and gone.

Chloe Richardson rubbed at her temples, seated at her desk in her fourth-floor office, which overlooked the bustling city draped in holiday glory.

It was the day after Thanksgiving and already every doorway had a charity-collecting Santa, trees were adorned in lights, and windows were decorated with items that everyone stood on the sidewalk and admired but could never afford.

Chloe had found herself standing outside the Tiffany store on her way into the office that morning, eyeing a bracelet she'd certainly put on the top of her list for Santa.

Tapping her pen against the contract that sat on her desk, she realized that it was just a few days into the holiday season but she wasn't feeling the spirit of the holidays, which was already encompassing the city. Usually, as was her tradition, she pulled out her Christmas tree, the box of lights, and the box of ornaments, which had been handed down, the day before Thanksgiving. She would decorate her tiny apartment until it glowed. That way, when she returned home from her parents' house after Thanksgiving, she was ready to celebrate Christmas. After all, having been born and raised in Aubrey Heights, which annually turned into a quaint Christmas village—tourists and all—there were some expectations as to what Christmas should look like, and Chloe took pride in that.

Being as organized as she was, shopping was usually done by the end of October, and the UPS delivery man was her favorite man in a uniform.

However, this holiday season—the entire fourth quarter actually—had taken her holiday spirit and thrown it right into the trash.

Since the end of September, she had been in that cramped little office nearly sixty hours a week. There had been no time to search Amazon for the perfect gifts, and worst of all, she'd missed Thanksgiving with her family. That was the straw that nearly broke the camel's back, she thought as she flipped through the pages of the contract that had now come back to her for a fifth revision.

She'd been asked to work on Wednesday, which was usually her set-up day and travel evening. Fine, she could reschedule the set-up of her decor, but when she hadn't even left the office at seven the night before Thanksgiving, all was lost.

Her mother, the trooper that she was, had simply said, "I'll put the turkey in the fridge, and we'll cook it on Saturday."

Now, as she sat at her desk at four o'clock on Friday afternoon, she wondered just how much longer she'd be sitting there before she could go home, pack, and figure out at what time she'd head out for the six-hour drive.

The headache pounding behind her eyes strengthened and she dropped her pen to her desk not wanting to see the words *herein* or *henceforth*.

What Chloe needed to remember was that she'd laid the groundwork to bring in a multi-million-dollar company to the tiny advertising agency. Now, just shy of turning thirty, she was in line for a hefty promotion—Account Manager.

By landing this new client, she was showing the owners of the firm that she was someone who could make things happen. Of course, she'd been showing them that for the past six years, knowing it would take time from the moment she was an intern.

Byron Mason, the owner of the firm, had been grooming her for the position since last Christmas. He knew her potential, but his son William, who had taken over the presidency of the company only a year ago, wasn't sold on a young woman executive. Even in today's society, there were still men who were just chauvinistic.

Still, she deserved the job, and no one in the entire company had landed a client as big as the one she was dealing with. All she had to do was get the contracts back to them and seal the deal. But now, in its fifth round of negotiations, she wondered if the contract would ever be finalized and if, in fact, she'd have a job the following week. For one year, it was worth missing Thanksgiving and not having a Christmas tree up and decorated. Next year, maybe her apartment would be bigger and she could have two trees. Yes, that would be a sign of success. That, and the bracelet in the *Tiffany* window. She'd make sure that little blue box was tucked under her tree. It would be a gift to her from herself for a job well done.

For the first time in days, Chloe laughed as she flipped through the contract one more time.

"What do you think? Did they sign off on everything yet?" Byron Mason walked through the door to her office. He'd aged considerably in the past six years, she thought as she looked up at the man who had a full head of white hair, a round body that was camouflaged by a custom-made suit, and a waddle to him that made her think of her grandfather.

"They added a few more stipulations, but I think we're almost there. I was just going over it one last time."

He smiled, which made his bushy white mustache wiggle. "May I have a seat?"

"Of course," she said, motioning to the chair in front of her desk. "Can I get you something to drink?"

"No. I'm headed out. The Mrs. made dinner reservations at the Plaza. I'm just waiting for her to call from the street and tell me she's here. No need to pay for parking."

"That sounds delightful."

"How was your Thanksgiving?"

Chloe forced herself to smile at the man. "It was quiet. I had a steak that I'd had in the freezer for a few months and some canned corn."

His bushy white brows drew together. "A meal for one?"

"Yes."

"You didn't go home?"

"I didn't have time this year. I'll head out early in the morning to drive to my parents' house. She saved dinner for me for the weekend."

As he pushed himself to his feet, he pointed at her. "I promise you'll never have to work this hard again. Next year, you'll be home for Thanksgiving. I promise."

"That's very kind. Thank you. Enjoy your dinner."

"I will," he said as he walked out of her office just as his son walked in.

"So? What's the verdict?"

Chloe swallowed hard as she looked up at the younger Mr. Mason, who was much taller than his father, thirty years younger, and much more straight forward.

"They added a few more clauses to the contract, and I'm finalizing that right now."

"Get on that, Ms. Richardson. I want to see final signatures on my desk on Monday."

"Yes, sir. I'll get these back to them right away so they can have legal go through it one more time."

"Monday," he restated as he walked out the door.

The headache she'd been nursing continued to throb, only now it had a new beat to it.

Pulling open her bottom drawer, she plucked out the Tylenol bottle and flipped off the lid. Pouring out two white pills, she popped them into her mouth and swallowed them down with the cup of cold coffee that sat on her desk.

"Excuse me," another voice came from the doorway. This time it was a younger man, exquisite suit, dark hair, and contrasting blue eyes that had Chloe choking on the bitterness of the coffee.

She coughed and covered her mouth as she tried to regain her composure, but the coughing wouldn't stop.

The man walked into her office and right to her desk. Now she could smell that his cologne was as exquisite as his suit.

"Here," he said as he pulled a bottle of water from his messenger bag. "I haven't opened it. I just picked it up in reception."

He handed it to her after twisting off the top.

Chloe took the bottle and sipped the water.

Grateful that it worked, she pushed away the fear that she was going to spit it all over him and damage his suit.

"Thank you." Her voice was raspy from the coughing. Once she'd caught her breath, and taken a few more sips of water, she looked up at the handsome stranger in her office. "Sorry for the rudeness."

"I didn't think you were rude," he said as he slung his messenger bag back over his shoulder. "I thought you were choking."

"I was."

He flashed her a smile that lit up those brilliant blue eyes. "Well, now that we have that all worked out, I wonder if you might be able to lead me to the office of Byron Mason. The receptionist wasn't at the desk out front, so I just came back."

"Oh, no problem. I'm not sure if he's still here, but we can go look. I know his son, William, is here."

Chloe stood from behind her desk to escort the man toward Byron's office. She expected him to just follow her, but he was shoulder to shoulder with her as they walked down the narrow corridor of the old building.

"I've met William," he said. "I was hoping to meet Byron before Monday."

"Are you only in town for a few days?" she asked, assuming that his rush to meet her boss meant he was leaving again.

"Oh, no. I live in the city. It's just good to get to know who you're working for before you start your new job."

That made her stop and turn to look at him. "New job? You're going to start working here?" Maybe it was some kind of Christmas miracle, she thought, inhaling that intoxicating cologne he wore.

"I am." He held out his hand to shake hers, and she took it. "Jason Mitchell."

"Chloe Richardson."

"Ah, your name was on my list of employees I'd be working with."

The smile was easy on her lips as she looked at him. Oh, Christmas miracle indeed. Santa had brought her a new glorious employee to look at while she took over the Account Manager position.

"So, we'll be working together?" she asked, realizing he still had a grip on her hand.

"Yes, I'm the new Account Manager, and I hear you've been a very busy bee this year bringing in some amazing accounts. I can't wait to see what this next year will bring."

She knew the smile had slipped from her lips, and now she could feel that headache pounding between her ears again. Had he seriously just said he was the Account Manager?

Those brilliant blue eyes were dull now as she dropped her hand to her side.

"Oh, Jason," William's voice echoed through the hallway. "You made it. My father just slipped out, but I convinced my mother to up her reservation for dinner, so we will join them. Let's chat in my office."

Chloe didn't want to turn and face William. She didn't want to know if he had a smug little smile going on or if he was absolutely clueless.

"Chloe," Jason said capturing her attention again. "It was very nice to meet you. I look forward to seeing you on Monday."

"Monday," she stammered. "Nice to meet you."

She stood there as he walked around her and a moment later she heard the door to William's office close.

Account Manager. She'd been completely bypassed for the job she'd been killing herself for. Did Byron Mason even know what his son had done?

Quickly she walked back to her office and kicked the door shut. If she made it home for her suitcase in the next hour, she'd head out of town right away. She could use a good dose of turkey dinner and time with her mother now. Maybe, just maybe, she wouldn't even come back to work on Monday. Maybe the Account Manager could find another puppet to bring in new clients.

She looked down at the contract on her desk, picked it up, and sent it right through the shredder.

A moment later, she shut the lights off in her office and headed out for a late Thanksgiving weekend.

CHAPTER 2

*E*ven if she was a grown woman, Chloe couldn't help but call her mother to tell her she was headed her way and to expect her around one in the morning.

There was concern on the other end of the phone, and that had been expected, but her mother's voice carried a cheery tone when she said she'd wait up for her.

That only made Chloe feel guilty for heading out of town in such a fever. She could have gone home, poured herself a glass of wine and slept off her mad before she trekked six hours in the dark and cold. There had been a few roads that still had snow packed on them, and others were dry. At the halfway mark, she stopped for gas, just as her father always would when they'd drive into the city. She, however, passed up the opportunity to buy one of the attached restaurant's signature cinnamon rolls, which were *World Famous*.

Christmas songs played on the radio as she moved from city to city. The drive reminded her of the scene in *Sleepless in Seattle* when Meg Ryan's character first hears Tom Hanks' character on the radio.

The thought had her giggling to herself, and that felt better than being mad. What if this little trip of hers ended up setting her on a journey away from her job to find the love of her life, just as it had for Meg Ryan's character.

Then the giggles stopped and the tired set in—and then the mad was back.

She'd killed herself to get the contract that she'd shredded—and that, too, made her mad. She was going to have to cut her trip short so she could get back in time, reprint the contract, and redline it again before anyone knew she'd never gotten it back to the client. Perhaps she could do that from her mother's house. She brought her laptop after all, because even mad to the point that she considered never returning, she was a professional who, up until that afternoon, loved her job. Her laptop went everywhere because she never knew when the opportunity to win over a new client might happen.

It had worked that way with *Pop! Cosmetics*, the new client she'd brought to the firm. Gloria Vandenberg was a young, up-and-coming fashion icon who had been compared to Coco Chanel. At only twenty-five, she had taken her inheritance from the *Vandenberg Furniture Company* and started *Pop! Cosmetics*. Hollywood elite were her spokespeople on social media. Having grown up in the upper crust society, she had some influential friends.

By chance, Chloe had met Gloria at a wine tasting event four months earlier for another client. Wasn't it lucky that William was much too busy to attend, so he'd sent Chloe. She and Gloria had hit it off with small talk, and that had moved into their love of romance novels, *Hallmark* movies, and sushi. A week later they were having dinner together at another event, and a week after that Gloria officially launched her up-and-coming empire.

Now that she was set to be in the major retailers, she wanted to get her name out beyond the teenagers and twenty-something women who watched social media. It was time to go big, but with a firm that was small enough to let her be part of everything. *Mason Arts, Inc* was exactly the kind of advertising firm Gloria was looking for, and Chloe Richardson was just the kind of woman she wanted to work with.

Chloe's father had taught her to keep it all personable, even when negotiating million-dollar deals. Above all else, people wanted personable.

It was easy for her to be herself around Gloria, even though Gloria was larger than life. She figured her dad was right. Chloe being herself was just what Gloria needed in her own life, and it was paying off.

So how come it paid off to pick up a million-dollar account, but it wasn't enough to secure the Account Manager position? Why had they brought in that Jason guy? What were his qualifications? Why did he get the job? And why didn't they even consider her for it?

She slapped the steering wheel. This man vs woman crap should be over by the twenty-first century. Equal pay for equal work and titles that go with it. The whole thing made her want to scream—and so she did. In the confines of her aging Subaru, she screamed.

Tears pooled in her eyes and so she screamed again. She screamed until it became laughter and the tears were secondary to the giggles that came next.

Screw the Mason family if they couldn't see what they had. Chloe Richardson was an up-and-comer too. Maybe she would talk to Gloria about a position inside *Pop! Cosmetics*.

The thought appealed to her more than she could have imagined. Maybe it was time to leave one side of advertising and move to another.

What if she were the one calling the shots from the other side of the table? What if she told Jason how she wanted things to work, and not taking direction from him?

As she passed the sign that told her she'd made it all the way to the quaint little town of Aubrey Heights, Chloe's mad was gone. Opportunity rang in her ears and fueled warmth in her blood.

Now with dry eyes, and an easy rhythm in her heart, she took a moment to slow her drive down Main Street and take in the visual glory of the twinkling lights in the bare trees. Christmas was always celebrated in Aubrey Heights in a special way. It always snowed on Christmas Eve, and from the Friday after Thanksgiving, Santa would walk the streets and greet everyone.

Tourists poured into the small community to visit their unique shops and restaurants. It was a drive from any major metropolitan area, but it was worth it.

People wanted to feel the magic of Christmas, and that's what they got when they visited.

There had been many times when Chloe wondered why she'd left the safe comforts of Aubrey Heights for the big city. Even now, when she was considering approaching Gloria Vandenberg about a job, which no doubt would steal all of her free time, she wondered why she didn't just move back and soak in the small town atmosphere permanently.

Then she remembered, nothing big happened in Aubrey Heights except Christmas magic, and that only came once a year.

Fine, she'd accept that, and she'd absorb all the

magic she could while she was there for the weekend. She could use a dose of Christmas and the joy that it seemed to bring to the masses.

No one could steal her joy unless she let them—and she'd let them for far too long. It was time for a change.

As she pulled up in front of the house where she'd been raised, she parked the car and sat for a moment in the wintry silence.

Who knew all she needed was a long drive to change her life? Now to sleep on it and see if she would feel the same way in the morning when she wasn't so tired, and so emotionally frazzled.

The porch light turned on and she saw her mother open the door and wave.

She was home, and for at least a day, she'd be loved, protected, and encouraged by the people who meant the most to her. That was all she needed.

CHAPTER 3

*T*he city still buzzed outside Jason's apartment window as he looked over the reports he'd managed to talk William Mason into giving him so that he could familiarize himself more with the company.

He'd taken a leap of faith when he accepted the position of Account Manager with the firm, but in meeting some of the staff and Byron Mason himself, he sure hadn't felt welcome. So why had William hired him?

The company was rumored to be picking up some sizable accounts. He'd heard that Gloria Vandenberg was considering signing with them, with a starting million-dollar advertising budget. To a company the size of *Mason Arts, Inc*, that was a big deal.

Mason Arts had made their name in the industry by working with the local community. Of course, the local community was millions of people. There was plenty of revenue to go around. They were one of the financial leaders in smaller agencies, which was what appealed to Jason.

He'd worked for the big agencies. He'd landed and worked multi-million-dollar deals. Cars, hotels, insurance, and of course *Vandenberg Furniture* all had been sold through his management. He knew why William Mason wanted him to be part of *Mason Arts*, but he felt as though he had nothing to offer.

William had told him he wanted to double the size of the agency as his father aged out of working, but after having had dinner with the man and his wife, Jason didn't get the feeling that Byron Mason was on the same page with his son.

He'd built his empire, and he didn't have any thoughts on retiring or making it so big it was unmanageable. They did millions in revenue a year, and by the looks of the reports, Chloe Richardson was responsible for bringing in most of those clients.

Sitting back in his chair behind the old desk that once was his father's, he tossed the papers he'd been studying onto the pile he'd been going through. So, why had the Masons not offered her the Account Manager position? Or had she passed it over? Certainly she was an asset to the company. A tug on the corner of his lips made him realize he was thinking about her in a different way too.

She was cute, he thought. Yeah, cute with her dark hair pulled back in a tail, and in a tailored business suit, sitting at her desk sipping her coffee. Her bitter coffee, he corrected his thought when he thought about the face she made as she choked on it as he made his presence known.

Jason chuckled as he looked at the clock. It was nearly two o'clock in the morning, and funny enough, he wondered what Chloe Richardson was doing at two o'clock on a Saturday morning. Was she going over reports, too? It wouldn't surprise him, especially if she was working on landing the *Pop! Cosmetics* account.

Leaning in toward his desk, he shuffled through

the papers until he found a sheet of notes he'd taken while sitting with William. He'd collected the phone numbers of his team, including Chloe Richardson's.

Maybe he'd call her just to say hi. Wouldn't that surprise her?

He chuckled again. Then again, it might not go over well if she wasn't a night owl.

Jason turned off his desk lamp and stood. Giving in to the much needed stretch, he let out a groan. He needed to learn to go to bed earlier. He took the time to make it to the gym and even plan out his meals on Sunday, so why couldn't he seem to get to bed at a reasonable hour?

For some reason, he took Chloe's phone number with him. He'd resigned to not call her, but he took it anyway. Intraoffice relationships were forbidden in his mind, especially between management and their team. But it never meant he couldn't enjoy working with her and striking up a friendship.

Oh, she might just be a horrible woman, and he was just lonely. That thought humored him, too, as he walked through his living room and turned off the lamp on the side table. Why was he even thinking about her? There were four other people that made up that team, but she was the only one he'd met. She'd be the only one on Monday morning that could call him by name.

Then again, she might think of another name for him. She had seemed rather surprised when he said he was the new Account Manager.

* * *

CHLOE'S MOTHER poured each of them a cup of tea, even though Chloe had told her to go to bed. It wasn't like her to simply open the door to her daughter and say, "I'll see you in the morning." Eveline Richardson was attentive. Besides, she knew her daughter well enough that if she missed Thanksgiving dinner, there was a reason, and if she'd driven all night long, there was a reason.

Her mother sat down at the table across from her and stirred milk into her cup, and then added sugar.

Chloe watched, and appreciated the process it as much as her mother staying up hours past her bedtime to be a comfort to Chloe. She also knew that her mother would never ask her what was troubling her, or tsk at anything Chloe might say. They could sit there for an hour, and conversation would only start when Chloe couldn't handle it any longer and spilled whatever was on her mind. It was like a drug, and Chloe was all in. She knew the rules, and she knew the results. And just like that, Chloe cracked before her mother's sugar was even dissolved in her cup.

"Before I left, I met the new Account Manager," Chloe said as her mother tapped a spoon to the side of her cup and then laid it to rest on the saucer.

"Account Manager. What do they do?"

"They manage the accounts for the firm. They are well versed in what the client needs and have earned the position by bringing in some of the biggest accounts, therefore their best interest is in overseeing them with a staff."

Her mother nodded as she lifted her cup to her lips and took a sip. "Who is this new manager?"

"Some guy named Jason," she spat out his name. "The point is, I met the guy who was hired when they passed me over for the promotion."

Now her mother's eyes rose to meet hers as she sipped her tea again. This time, she set the cup back on the saucer and reached for Chloe's hand. "Sweetheart, I'm sorry to hear that. Why did they do that?"

"I don't know. I was right in the middle of finalizing a million-dollar contract—a million-dollar contract," she repeated. "He came in, dropped his name and new position, and was whisked away to dinner with the president and his family."

"They didn't give you reason?"

She shook her head and then took a sip of her own tea to calm herself. "I didn't get a chance to ask yet. It all went so quickly. All I know is I've been killing myself for that firm since I was an intern. I've brought in millions of dollars in revenue in those years, and now I'm landing one of their biggest clients. So what do they do? They hire someone else to manage it."

Her mother sat with a thoughtful look. "Maybe it's a sign. You know when a door closes, and a window opens. This is your window. You'll bring in the client, and there will be a bigger promotion for you, or a new opportunity."

"Yeah, well I'm thinking of not going back on Monday. See how they like that. And, I brought in that client, which we haven't finalized the contracts on. I could easily persuade her to go to another firm. In fact," her voice was growing in pitch and volume, "I've even thought about asking Gloria Vandenberg if she'd hire me internally to manage the account from the other side."

The more she said it aloud, the more she liked the idea.

"Gloria Vandenberg, like in *Vandenberg Furniture?*"

"The granddaughter. She inherited a great sum of money when her grandfather died and they sold off the stores. She took her inheritance and opened *Pop! Cosmetics.* They compare her to Coco Chanel."

"I will look for it the next time I go to the store. Admirable of her to do something big and bold."

"Exactly. I happened to meet her at a function, and now she's considering a million-dollar ad campaign through our company. And I brought that to the table."

"But they hired this other person?"

"Yes."

"Did they promise you the job?"

"Mom, I was being groomed for the job. I've worked for years for that position."

"But they didn't say it was yours."

She thought about it. "It's worked that way since I was an intern. Whenever the position opened up, then the associate that brought in the most accounts and actively managed them at the associate level got the job."

"Until today?"

Chloe let out a deflated breath. "Yes, until today."

"That's a shame, sweetheart. You should talk to them on Monday and tell them about your disappointment. Maybe they didn't even know you wanted the job."

How could they not have known? She'd talked to Byron about it, but her mother's words echoed in her ears. He hadn't actually said the job was hers.

And this was the point in the evening where her mother would leave her with her cup of tea and her thoughts, which was exactly what she did.

Her mother kissed her atop the head. "I'll make waffles in the morning for you. Turkey goes in early, so rest up. You can nap later."

She watched as her mother walked down the hallway toward her bedroom and disappeared. And just like that, Chloe was alone with her thoughts, which were now completely different. Instead of being mad, she was embarrassed for thinking that they'd simply hand over the promotion to her.

CHAPTER 4

*S*ub-zero wind chill made Jason's morning ritual run nearly intolerable, but he'd done it and checked it off his to-do list. Now, as he warmed up with a cup of coffee, he watched the Saturday morning news.

Usually, he'd head into town and spend a few quiet hours in his office, but since he was in the middle of a job change, he didn't really have any work to do. Perhaps he should go through the three boxes he'd carted out of his last office and decide what was even relevant. He supposed he could go in and get organized.

When his phone rang, he saw his sweet mother's face pop up on the screen, and it instantly brought a smile to his face.

"Hello, Mother," he said as he answered.

"You sound chipper."

"I just got back in from a run. It's frigid out there."

He heard her sigh, which was a combination of disbelief and slight irritation. "You are going to give yourself a heart attack just like your father did."

"I'm hoping to avoid the heart attack."

She laughed now. "Well, while you're freezing in the city, I am sitting poolside with a drink. I guess we have always had a difference of opinion when it comes to lifestyle."

"We most certainly have." He laughed too.

His mother lived in Palm Beach, in a retirement community full of people, just like her, who hated snow. The moment his father had died, from that inevitable heart attack, she had packed up her belongings and headed for the sun. Jason, he liked the difference in weather. The frigid cold and the unbearable heat, those were signs of passage when he survived them each year.

He enjoyed visiting his mother and sitting by the pool with a cocktail. But that wasn't his kind of lifestyle. He was a workaholic, and he admitted it. The bustle of the city gave him energy.

"Are you coming down here for Christmas?" she asked, before he heard her sipping her drink.

"Well, I start a new job on Monday. I don't know how flexible my holidays are going to be."

"Jason, we didn't have Thanksgiving together. I didn't make a big deal about it, but I really thought we'd have Christmas together." Her voice carried sadness, which always in turn filled him with guilt.

"I'll know more after I start on Monday. And, if I have to fly to Florida on Christmas morning, and fly out that night, I will do it."

He heard the gratified sigh. "That's my boy. Tell me about your new job."

He told her what he knew of it. Of course, she was impressed by its title. She didn't understand the business of advertising, but she bragged to everyone she knew that her son was part of it. When watching TV with her, she would always ask him if he was in charge of that ad or this ad. Sometimes, he'd just say yes to a grand ad, even if it wasn't his. After all, she didn't understand anyway.

What he didn't share with her was the doubt he had already about his new job. The look on Chloe Richardson's face still haunted him. Sure, he was as ruthless as they came. He would go after any account to make money, but to have taken somebody's job, that wasn't his style.

He knew what it was to work hard for a position. He'd done it many times. The thrill of a new job, that always had him too. But he knew Chloe had been with the company since she graduated college. Most of the accounts had her name on them. So why had they hired him?

Maybe they knew something he didn't know. Perhaps Chloe was planning on moving. Did she have a new job somewhere else? Had she thought someone else was going to get the job and she was disappointed? Perhaps what bothered him even more, was that he didn't know why he cared.

* * *

Chloe had been awakened by the smell of waffles and the sound of conversation coming from the kitchen. She wasn't completely surprised to find her father, mother, aunt, and cousin all in the kitchen when she walked in.

Her father rose when he saw her, and without a word, he wrapped his arms around her and squeezed. The sensation filled her with a warmth that she knew she would carry back to the city with her.

"Hey, peanut," he said as he eased back and took a long look at her. "She looks fine, Evie."

So, also to be expected, her mother was calm in front of her, but she'd worried aloud to Chloe's father.

"I said she looked tired. Don't go making me sound like a worry-wart."

Chloe's aunt Janice stood and hugged her tightly as well. "You look good. How is big city life?"

"It's good. It keeps me busy and very social."

"That's good then."

Her cousin Roz hugged her next. The much younger Richardson only smiled at her when they pulled apart.

"How's college?" Chloe asked.

"Hard. Harder than I thought it would be."

"You're a freshman. It'll get harder, but you'll get tougher, too."

"My roommate is a slut."

Chloe held in the laugh that wanted to break free, and Roz was too busy to notice Chloe's expression when Roz's mother smacked her on the shoulder.

"I have a plate of waffles for you right here." Chloe's mother handed her the plate and shooed everyone out of her way to sit down.

Chloe sat down at the table and her father excused himself to the other room to catch a football game. Roz, phone in hand and head down, followed him. She was left alone with her mother and aunt, and she could tell they both wanted to chat.

"Mom, I miss your waffles in the mornings."

"I'll send you home a bag so you can freeze them."

Chloe expected no less. Each time she visited, she went home with a bag of waffles, frozen spaghetti sauce, and whatever frozen vegetable her mother had a bumper crop of that summer.

"Any new men in your life?" Janice asked and even

Chloe's mother shifted her aunt a look of confusion. "Seriously, you're almost thirty, I just thought I'd ask."

"I have a lot of thirty-plus friends who don't have a man in their life."

"That's the city talking."

Maybe it was, but Chloe wasn't looking for a man.

CHAPTER 5

$\mathcal{T}$he glory of having Thanksgiving dinner on a Saturday was that Chloe could head into town and shop the stores that lined Main Street. She'd been given explicit instructions to be back by two o'clock.

She'd yet to tell her mother that she was going to head back to the city as early as six the next morning so that she could work that contract for *Pop! Cosmetics*. No matter what her employment status was the following day, her conscience said that she needed to do what was right. She trusted the team at *Mason Arts*, so there was no reason not to continue with the contract.

She'd come to that conclusion while her mother and aunt discussed Roz's ever-changing hair color, her father's knee problems, and the neighbor's cat, had seemed to ease the tension Chloe was feeling. Tomorrow she would walk into her office and conduct herself in the same manner that she always did. When the entire staff was introduced to the new Account Manager, she would be cordial. And, when it was said and done, she would go directly to Byron Mason and ask why. Depending on his answer, she would either work very hard to bring in the next big client, or she'd have exactly two weeks left to work for *Mason Arts* and she'd be sending out resumes.

Stopping into the first store on the street, Chloe was greeted by name and that brought a smile to her face. Her friend from high school, Melanie Peet, owned the store.

"You look fantastic," Melanie said as she pulled Chloe in for a hug and then held her at arm's length to get a good look at her. "You just look great."

"Well, thank you. You look well too, and your store is beautiful."

Melanie looked around and admired it for herself. "It's a dream come true. You know how I always wanted a store filled with pretty things. Now I have one."

"You sure do."

"What can I help you find? Are you Christmas shopping?"

"I'm just looking really. I didn't make it for Thanksgiving dinner, so Mom has it in the oven now."

"That's sweet."

"I would like to get her a little something though. What would you recommend?"

Melanie pursed her lips in thought. "Are you thinking something personal, like bath salts or lavender soap? I have a nice gift basket with lotions too. Or maybe some handcrafted earrings. Those are a hot item now, too."

"Let's look at the earrings. That sounds fun."

Melanie had showed her a perfect pair of ear-rings, wrapped them, and was sending Chloe on her way.

With a smile on her face, and a sample of fudge between her frozen fingers, Chloe walked down the street where every window was decorated for Christmas.

Oh, the windows in the city were infamous for their decorations, but nothing beat a small town at Christmas—nothing. Chloe thought it looked like a painting. The streets and trees were covered in snow. Red bows and wreaths hung from the lampposts. The Christmas windows and bundled shoppers added to the mystique. Christmas music was piped through the town, and she could smell chestnuts from the little cart that appeared on Saturdays during the holidays. People wrote books and movies about places like Aubrey Heights. And it was insightful times like this that Chloe wondered why she'd ever left.

Would she be happy like Melanie Peet selling soaps and earrings? What about serving people coffee every day in a quaint coffee shop?

No, her mind just didn't work that way. The bustle of the city drew her in too. The noise from her apartment window. The small specialty shops where she did her grocery shopping instead of the local grocery store, that had a pull. She was glad she'd been raised somewhere simple like Aubrey Heights. It made her appreciate the entire world.

She had made it to the end of the street when her cell phone rang. Admittedly she was surprised to see Gloria's face pop up on the screen.

"Gloria, how are you?" Chloe asked as she crossed the street and headed toward the coffee shop.

"Chloe, I was waiting on those contracts. I thought I'd have them last night."

The festive feeling drained from Chloe's chest. "Yes, you should have had them."

"I'm sure it was the courier. They are never reliable."

Guilt twisted in her gut. "I will hand deliver them to your office on Monday morning."

She heard the sigh on the other end of the phone. "That's why I want to work with you. The personal attention to detail. I just can't get that anywhere else."

Right. That personal attention to detail. "I'll take care of it."

"Wonderful. Did you go home for the weekend? You'd mentioned a late Thanksgiving."

Had she? She must have felt comfortable enough to talk about personal things, which in business, she tried not to do. Though, sometimes it was nice to have a friend who wasn't in the same business, because in the city, all she knew were people with the same interests.

The thought bummed her out a bit. How had she gotten so stale?

"Yes, I'm home for the weekend. My mother has the turkey in the oven right now. I'm walking through town and soaking in the Christmas spirit."

"Sounds heavenly. Sister, I have to go. But you get me those contracts on Monday, and we'll get to work. In fact, bring them by about eight-thirty and I'll cater in breakfast."

And then there were the perks. "I'll be there at eight-thirty."

"Ciao!" Gloria said before the line went dead.

Chloe rubbed the ache that had started between her brows. Now she had to head back to the city, go to the office, pull up the contracts, and redo them. And that all had to be done on Sunday. Her mother was not going to be happy.

* * *

GOING through the boxes that he'd brought from his

last office, Jason couldn't believe the crap he'd collected over the years. Seriously, why did someone need a magic eight ball, a Slinky, a stress ball that looked like a little yellow man, and a paper weight that looked like someone cut off a piece of metal and left it on his desk. He didn't have enough paperwork and computer parts on that desk, he needed trinkets too?

He'd almost narrowed down all the things to one box that he could take with him on Monday morning and put in his office. It would make him look more professional, and it would be a little more homey that way too. And, if he didn't come up with anything better to do tomorrow, he'd go in and set everything up. Why not? William had given him a key to the building and elevator, as well as his new corner office.

As he sat on the floor of his home office, his phone rang. The picture that came up on the screen had him holding off on answering. Deborah King's long blonde hair and those deep blue doe eyes stared at him as the incessant buzzing echoed. He hadn't told her that he'd left the firm. Surely she'd find out on Monday with the rest of the staff—only she might take it personally, and she should.

Her advances, innuendos, and temper tantrums had made working at the firm too hard. He felt like a wuss for even thinking it, but men could be manipulated too, and that's what Deborah had done to him.

She'd used him to get a promotion, to wiggle her way into claiming accounts, and all under the veil of a relationship.

No more. He would never do that to someone, and he'd never let it happen to him again. There was no room for relationships in the workplace.

Mason Arts was a fresh start for him. There was no

looking back. Deborah could call his phone as much as she wanted, but he wasn't going to answer.

He winced when it alerted him that he had a voice message.

Setting his phone on his desk, he rose from the floor, and walked toward the kitchen to make a sandwich. He'd get to the message when he was ready, not a moment before. Right now, he just wanted the silence within his apartment.

CHAPTER 6

*I*t was still dark when Chloe drove out of Aubrey Heights with a latte in the cup holder and Christmas music on the radio. She wasn't sure if she should be upset that she had to leave at the ungodly hour of six in the morning to get back to the city, or that her mother didn't seem all that surprised that she was heading out.

What did that say about Chloe? People expected her to miss holidays or hurry in and hurry out. That wasn't the person she wanted to be. But there was no way around it, not now. She'd worked her tail off to get the *Pop! Cosmetics* account, she sure as hell wasn't going to hand it over to be run without her. But then again, wasn't that what she was thinking when she shredded the damn contract?

It wasn't until the sirens behind her blared that she realized her head was in the clouds and she was well exceeding the posted speed limit sign on the side of the highway. Perhaps she was in a bigger hurry to get back to the city than she'd thought.

To make matters worse, when she rolled down the driver's side window to speak to the officer, she instantly recognized the face.

"Well, well, well. Chloe Richardson. It seems as if you're in a hurry to leave our part of the world every time you visit."

Of course it would seem that way. This would be her third ticket from Officer Johnson—Officer Curt Johnson, ex-boyfriend from high school.

"Hey, Curt. My head was somewhere else I guess."

"That's going to get you or someone else killed. License and registration."

"Do you really need that? You know who I am. You know I've owned this car forever."

The smirk on his face didn't ease. "License and registration."

Reluctantly, she pulled the items from her purse and glovebox and handed it to him.

"Where you going so fast?"

"I have a big contract I need to work on in the city. I was thinking about that as I was driving."

"In a big hurry to get it done?"

"You have no idea," she said in nearly a whisper. "I'll slow it down."

Curt nodded. "I still have to run these. It'll just be a minute." He turned and walked back to his car.

She watched as the cabin of the car illuminated when he turned on the overhead light. Anyone within a mile of the highway knew someone had been pulled over with the lights flashing into the dark woods.

She could have nearly calculated, to the minute, how long it would take him to get back to her. By the time he had, she'd nearly sipped down her entire latte and could certainly use a bathroom.

"You're clear to go," he said as he handed her back her license and registration, along with the ticket he'd written up. "You can just pay the fine. No need to come back and zip through town to go to court."

He had the upper hand here, and she knew he liked that little bit of authority. "Thanks."

"Take it slow," he drawled out the words as he walked back to his car and waited for her to pull away.

There was a reason she'd chosen to go to college in the city and get out of town. There was something to be said about being anonymous when you went somewhere every day. It wouldn't be even dinner time before her mother called and scolded her about the ticket. News, even though it was only between her and Curt at this point, would travel fast.

Minding the speed, and the need to pee, she turned up the music and headed toward the next town at the correct speed. She'd be damned if he got the satisfaction of stopping her again.

* * *

SUNDAYS in an empty office had always been one of Jason's favorite times. All business—all to himself.

He was a bit of a glutton that way. He liked his work. Early mornings, late at nights, and weekends were when he thrived. During the day he got caught up in watching the masses work. Everyone had a different method—a different style. There was the meeting maker who just loved to organize people into one place at one time. How many meetings had he been to where nothing had been covered? Then there was the one with the day planner in hand who had everything color coordinated. Did they spend more time on highlighting things than they did on the actual events? His favorite was the chaos organized. The people who had papers all over their desk, looked as if they'd been tasered, and yet knew right where everything was—those were the people he enjoyed the most. They weren't looking for his approval, they were there to get a job done.

He supposed, in a sense, he was the latter of the organized, however, usually being the supervisor or boss, he had to look like the color-coordinated person. Maybe that was why he liked working when everyone else was gone. He could live in his chaos and no one could see it.

As he went over the list of potential new clients that William had provided him with, he heard the sound of the elevator and a door. Maybe he wasn't the only person who coveted Sundays in the office.

Pushing back from his desk, he slowly walked to his office door and listened again. Yes, someone was on the floor, and it didn't sound like housekeeping.

He walked along the corridor flanked with windowed offices and cubicles. His sneakers made no noise on the carpet. There had been no fear that it might be an intruder, as someone would have had to have the key to the elevator to arrive on the floor.

As he turned the corner, he noticed the light in the office closest to the reception area. The office where he'd met Chloe on Friday.

Giving it some thought as he slowly and quietly moved toward her office, he took her as the color-coded type of organizer. Yeah, she was no nonsense and ready to take over the world.

He was glad she was there. It would give them some time to get to know one another. Maybe he could get some insight as to why she'd looked so frazzled when he'd introduced himself as the Account Manager.

Jason turned the corner to her office, a smile at the ready, and friendly conversation lined up in his mind as a stapler flew through the air nailing him right in the forehead.

He stumbled back, hitting one of the walls of a nearby cubicle before falling to the floor with blood dripping in his eye from where he'd collided with the stapler.

"Oh-my-God!"

He heard the trembling voice before he saw the fuzzy image of the woman in yoga pants and an oversized sweat shirt kneeling down in front of him.

"I'm sorry. I'm so sorry." She stood, knocking her knee into his side as she tore tissues from a box on a random desk and pressed them to his head. "I never have anyone in here on Sundays. I didn't know anyone was here. I saw you lurking, and…"

"I wasn't lurking."

"You were lurking." She sat down next to him on the floor. "I think I should take you to emergency care. You might need stitches."

"It'll be a tale for tomorrow, that's for sure," he said as he tried to sit up and steady himself. "I'm sorry I scared you."

"Seriously, I'm sorry. I'm all worked up, and I've been on the road for hours, I'm a little punchy. Where's your coat? I'll take you for stitches."

Jason's head pounded, but he couldn't help but use that smile he'd been saving as he looked up at her.

Her brown hair was tossed up in one of those messy buns, and she had no makeup on. The sweat-shirt said Aubrey Heights High School on it, and it had been worn many, many times. She looked much different than the uptight professional he'd met on Friday. Maybe it was the injury to his head, but something stirred in him to want to kiss her.

CHAPTER 7

*H*e was bleeding and smiling at her. Chloe sat on the floor staring at the man, who was now her boss, and thinking he'd been injured so much he didn't realize he had blood running down his cheek.

"I'll get your coat. Do you have your wallet? I'll pay for the stitches. This is my fault."

He was still smiling at her as he pulled the wad of tissues from his forehead and looked at them.

"You really think I need stitches?"

As the next trickle of blood dripped from the hole she'd left on his head, she reached up for more tissue and pressed it to his forehead. "Yes. I've seen cuts like that before. You'll need a few stitches."

"Well, I have nothing else going on today. Let's go."

He was delusional, she thought as they managed to both stand while she continued to hold the tissues to his head.

"Here, hold this." She took his hand and put it over the tissues. "I'm going to get your coat. If you get dizzy, find a chair."

"I'm fine."

She wasn't sure about that because he was still smiling.

Chloe ran to the corner office, which she'd coveted, and found his coat hanging on the rack by the door. Looking around, she didn't see a pair of boots, and she could feel his gloves in the pockets of the coat.

She hurried back to where he now sat on the edge of a desk. Chloe searched for blood that might have gotten on the floor, or on the desk. The woman who sat there would pass out if she saw even a drop of dried blood anywhere around her workspace.

"Let's get this on you." She held out the coat so he could slip his arms in easily, and she noted the scent of cologne that lingered in the fabric. It was intoxicating, she thought as he shrugged it on, always with one hand on the tissue on his head.

"I'll get my coat and we'll head out. There's an urgent care around the corner," she said as she hurried into her office and pulled out her cap from the pocket of her coat.

"When did they decide every corner needed an urgent care like a 7-11? I mean, do people get hurt that often?"

She listened to him ramble as she put on her coat and gloves. "Maybe workers are always throwing things at their bosses' heads."

He laughed at that, but she didn't think it was funny. If William was trying to push her out by hiring someone else, her attacking him was probably going to seal the deal. And, even worse, now she wasn't going to get the contracts to Gloria on time if they didn't get his head stitched up and get back to the office. But really, how many people could be at urgent care on a Sunday afternoon?

. . .

Jason was sure that he'd bleed out before they could take him back and stitch up his head. A nurse had given him a gauze pad to replace the tissue that had dried to his skin.

Chloe sat next to him frantically filling out his medical record in her beautiful penmanship.

"Address?"

He gave it to her and watched as she made perfect fours.

"Phone number?"

She wrote it down.

"I'm a Pisces. My favorite color is red. I like my pizza with just sausage, and I'm sensitive to gluten, but I can't keep away from it."

She stopped writing and looked up at him. "I don't think I need all that. But thanks," she snapped, but it only made it funnier to him.

"I just thought it was a good time to get to know each other. My turn, why don't you answer those questions for me?" He tried to smile, but each time he did it hurt his head.

"Everything you need to know about me is in my employee file. You can ask H.R. if you need to see it since you're my boss."

She directed her attention right back to the form, but he got the message loud and clear. She wasn't happy about his new position.

Chloe continued to ask pertinent information to finish the form, and he obliged with serious answers now. They could talk about her attitude toward him later when they went back to the office. He wasn't going to let some stitches and time away from his tasks at hand keep him from being productive.

Although he hadn't expected it to take them three and a half hours to finally be seen. He was sure his forehead was healed by the time the doctor came in and the nurse began to clean out the wound.

He'd seen Chloe's face go white when the doctor asked how the accident had happened. There was some relief when he told the doctor that he had a new job and was moving into his office when the box fell off a shelf and the stapler hit him in the head. He wasn't sure if he believed it, but it seemed to suffice, and helped to return color to Chloe's face.

Once the three stitches were secured, the nurse left the room to file the paperwork, which he was sure would cost him over a thousand dollars. He'd hate to admit it aloud, but it was worth a thousand dollars to get to know Chloe, even just a little bit.

"I'M SO sorry for all of this," Chloe said as she sat in the chair next to the bed, her hands folded tightly in her lap. "I'll pay the bill, too. This was all my fault."

"I spooked you. I deserve it."

She figured he deserved it. He was the S.O.B. who was taking her job after all, but she wasn't one to hurt people on purpose. Well, not since she'd gotten revenge on her friend Cat for pushing her in the mud in fifth grade.

"Wait till William finds out what I did. He'll have me searching for a job by noon," she said shaking her head.

Jason swung his legs over the side of the bed and caught her attention.

"This has nothing to do with William. He doesn't need to know what happened. This is between you and me. Someday, when I walk into your office, and you're stapling something, we'll both laugh. Some friendships start off rocky."

What the hell was that all about, she wondered as she sat back in her chair. "Friendships?"

"Sure. I don't have any friends at *Mason Arts*. It would be nice to show up to work on Monday and know a name, a face, have a laugh."

Crap! He wasn't the asshole she was pegging him to be. It would be much easier if she hated him, but she was finding out that the Pisces that liked the color red and ate pizza when it made him sick was an okay guy.

"Thanks," she said softly, trying to keep her composure. "You'll be very happy at the firm. They're wonderful to work for."

"And you're quite the producer. *Pop! Cosmetics*? How on earth did you land that for a firm as small as ours?"

Chloe wasn't sure he qualified to call the firm *ours* since he hadn't even started yet. But, then again, he was further up the ladder than she was now.

"I met Gloria Vandenberg at a networking event. We're close in age, and we hit it off. She wanted to give *Pop!* a fresh voice, and a small firm could do that."

"Genius. I didn't see the contracts on it yet, though."

Okay, maybe he was an asshole. He'd gotten her talking while they sat in the quiet, sterile room, and he dove right into business and what she was doing to earn her position.

"Malfunction with the shredder. I'm taking a new copy to her in the morning at eight-thirty. I'll be a little late getting to work in the morning."

"Nothing like a hand-delivered contract. Is there anything I can help you with when we get back to the office?"

No, she didn't want his help. She didn't want to

like him, and she was more comfortable wishing the stitches caused him some pain.

"I should have it ready to print within an hour."

He smiled, though she noticed it only reached his cheeks. She had to assume his forehead was still numb, and it made her chuckle.

"What kind of coffee do you drink?" Jason asked as he watched her muse to herself.

"Me? I don't drink coffee. Not a lot. Well, I do, but I prefer hot chocolate."

He considered her for a moment. "That has a lot of sugar."

"So do half the drinks people carry around in those white cups with that green mermaid on it."

"You think it's a mermaid?"

"I don't know," she said with a bite, growing irritated with the conversation. "None of this is relevant. I will be late in the morning because I'm delivering contracts. As soon as they let us out of here, I'm going back to the office to finish the contract and then I'm going home. I've had a long weekend, and I've driven for hours. I'm exhausted."

"Where did you drive from?" The corner of his mouth curled up when he asked.

"That won't be in my file."

Luckily the door opened and the stone faced nurse handed him a stack of papers and a bill for one-thousand, two-hundred and fifty dollars.

Even though guilt punched at her stomach, she felt as though he deserved it when he handed the woman taking payments his credit card.

CHAPTER 8

*S*he didn't like him, Jason decided as they rode the elevator in silence, and Chloe shut her office door without another word.

It wouldn't be the first time he had a woman in his office despise him just for having a penis. Then, on the other hand, Deborah King thought that was a reason to chase after him. He never claimed to understand women, and he supposed he never would.

He did, however, want Chloe Richardson to like him—as a human. Above all else, he was that—human. He might have moved in on her job, but he didn't know that when he'd talked to William about it. Neither Byron nor William Mason had mentioned that there was anyone in-house that was qualified or in line for the job.

Screw her if she harbored resentment against him. He was there to do a job, and damnit he was going to do the best job possible—but he'd need Chloe on his team.

She hadn't said she was going to quit or anything of the sort. There was no need to worry that she would take her talent for landing clients and move on. And even though she was very attractive, and he knew deep down she had a nice streak too, he was all business. He had to remind himself of that when he'd caught sight of her through her office window, head down working on the contract that had originally had a shredder incident. He'd want to know more about that.

For the time being, he was going to go back to his office, shut his door, turn up his music, and move in. T-minus fifteen hours and he was going to have a lot of new faces looking at him and whispering behind his back. It wasn't new to him, and he'd learned how to handle it. It would be interesting to see how Chloe Richardson handled it too.

* * *

MONDAY MORNING, with contract in hand, Chloe rode the glass elevator to the twenty-eighth floor and marveled when the doors opened to the bright pink wall that said *Pop! Cosmetics*. The genius behind the interior decor, and the bustling office gave her chills. She loved the energy. She loved the atmosphere. Even just being the smallest part of what could be the company's continued success fueled her.

She'd been in the offices numerous times, but she stopped by reception, signed in and awaited her pink name tag that alerted everyone that she was a visitor. After a ten minute wait in the lobby, and a hand-crafted latte from the barista in the corner, she was escorted back to Gloria Vandenberg's office by her assistant John-Paul.

"Can I get you anything while you wait? She'll be just a minute."

"I'm good," she said as she sat down.

He left her in the office with the door cracked open just a bit. It reminded her of a move her own mother would make when she was a child and she wanted to hear what was going on in the other room.

As usual, Gloria entered from another door. She was dressed in head-to-toe pink, which was bright and brilliant, and in stark contrast to Chloe's head-to-toe black suit.

"Chloe!" Gloria squealed as she moved toward her. Chloe stood and was enveloped in a hug, and was sure she'd smell Gloria's perfume the rest of the day.

"It's nice to see you, Gloria."

"Sit, sit. Did John-Paul offer you something to drink? He's supposed to."

Chloe sat back down. "I had a latte in the lobby."

"Fantastic, isn't it? I have to watch my weight working in this office."

"I have the contracts for you," Chloe offered, hoping to move the meeting right along. She pulled them from her bag and set them on Gloria's desk. "I have multiple copies if you want a set for legal."

Gloria's lips pursed. "I'll take them. Here's the deal, sweetheart. You know, if it was only me, I'd sign it in a minute. But, since I have VCs, they get some say."

"Right. As is expected."

"Well, there's more. Had I signed these on Friday, I would have stepped all over the VCs." She waved her hand in the air. "But this morning they had me meet with Deborah King from *Stockton Advertising*. Do you know Deb?"

Deb? That seemed a bit personal to Chloe, but she shook her head. "No, I don't know her."

"She's a feisty thing. Anyway, she just got promoted at the agency when some tool left. She has some solid ideas though. I do like your ideas, but, honey..."

It was all she had to say. Chloe's heart was in her throat and she did everything she could to not let the tears surface that desperately wanted to bust through.

"Business is business. I get that," she offered easing herself to the edge of her seat. "But you know we work well together. You'll have my one-on-one, un-divided attention. *Mason Arts* can handle your needs, and where else will you get the personal attention?"

"I know. I know." Gloria sat back in her chair and picked up her smartphone. "I'll let you know when legal is done with the contract. I'll talk you up, girl. You know I will."

And just like that, Chloe was dismissed.

* * *

JASON TRIED to scan the small group in the confer-ence room and remember everyone's names. He'd been introduced as they all came in for complimen-tary coffee and donuts. William Mason boasted about Jason's reputation in the industry, but Byron Mason acted as if they'd never met. He wondered if the elder Mason's health was slipping and that was why his son was taking the lead on so many projects.

He had noticed that Chloe still hadn't arrived at ten o'clock, but her meeting had been at eight-thirty. He was going to take it as a good sign that her meeting had run long. At least that's what he kept telling himself until he saw her come in off the ele-vator and go straight to her office, shutting the door behind her.

What he witnessed wasn't someone who had had a great and successful morning. No, she looked much as she had the day before when they'd returned from urgent care.

As everyone made their way back to their desks, Jason answered a few more questions and continued to walk down the hall toward Chloe's door.

A fiery redhead crossed in front of him and into the office before he could knock, and shut the door behind her.

Perhaps a later time, he thought as he continued to walk through the office attempting not to attract too much attention to himself.

By lunch time he hadn't seen Chloe emerge from her office, and the redhead had been in and out multiple times. A few conference calls, and a meeting dragged the day into afternoon, and he'd yet to see her come out of her office even once. Didn't the woman eat?

At five-thirty, the redheaded protector, whose name he thought was Kim or Kate or Allison, finally went home. The office began to empty and even both Byron and William had stopped by his door to say goodbye. By six-thirty, he thought he'd knock on her door.

He'd have hoped she'd bring him back signed contracts, but since the day had passed by and she hadn't even spoken to him, he was sure that was part of her hiding out. Well, there was no need for that. They'd been friendly the day before, they could be friendly again. Maybe he could use sympathy to get her attention. After all, the three dark knots of string on his forehead were all because of her.

he blinds were drawn on the window, but the light from her office spilled out into the hallway, which was now dark, but for the emergency lights.

Jason stayed alert, listening carefully to see if he could hear her, not wanting another set of stitches. Just as he lifted his hand to knock, the door flew open and Chloe ran right into him, knocking him back into the cubicle wall behind him.

"Do you freaking have a death wish?" she hollered as she stumbled back. "Dear, God! What the hell are you doing?"

"I came to say hello."

"Hello? It's six-thirty at night."

"And you haven't been out of your office all day," he reminded her as he fixed his suit jacket. "So, hello. How was your day?"

He didn't like the tone in his voice, but it seemed to match the scowl on her face.

"It's fine. Are we done here? I still have some work to do."

"Like you said, it's six-thirty. Don't you think you should call it a day? Get some dinner? Relax?"

Chloe fisted her hands and set them on her hips. "I don't work that way. I'll work until I'm done."

"And that's why you're an asset, but seriously, what's with the attitude? I haven't bothered you all day."

He watched as her shoulders dropped and she rested her hand on her stomach, which he was sure he'd heard growl.

"I'm sorry. I'm just a little punchy." She turned back to her office, walked back to her desk, and sat down behind it.

Jason followed. "How did your meeting go with *Pop! Cosmetics*? Or do I assume it didn't go well?"

Chloe dropped her head into her hands, her elbows rested on her desk. "I should have had them to her Friday, but it didn't work out just right."

"Problem with the shredder," he reminded her of her words.

"Something like that. Anyway, she would have signed them without another thought had I gotten them to her on Friday. But in the meantime, someone named Deborah King," she said with her hand waving in the air angrily, "had a meeting with her and has a lot to offer. I killed myself for this account. It didn't get me anywhere. I didn't get the promotion and I didn't land the client," she bit out the words.

Jason replayed her words in his head and decided it had shaken him enough he thought he'd sit down too.

"Deborah King moved in on this account?"

"*Deb*, Gloria called her." She let out a groan. "Yes, that's what I'm saying. I don't know who the hell she is, but she swooped right in."

"I'll bet she did."

He noticed Chloe perk right up when he said that. "So you know *Deb*?"

"You could say that."

"Ah, you know her well?"

He didn't like the insinuation, but it came with the territory as far as *Deb* was concerned.

"I know her well enough to have left a cushy six-figure job over her."

Humor lit in Chloe's eyes as she eased back in her chair. "Oh, do tell. I'd like someone else to fume over her too. I've spent some of my day googling her and can't get the image of her mug out of my head."

Jason couldn't help but laugh at that. "Why torture yourself like that?"

"Because it pissed me off." She pressed her hand to her stomach again.

"I'll tell you what. I'll spill all I know on *Deb* if you'll let me feed you. Have you eaten anything today?"

"Latte in the lobby of *Pop! Cosmetics.*"

"That was early this morning."

"Yeah. Jody brought me a donut and tried to feed me half of her turkey sandwich, but I just couldn't stomach it."

"Jody is the redhead?"

"Yeah."

He sucked at names, he decided. "What's nearby?"

"Anything. That's the glory of the city, right?"

He chuckled in agreement. "Deli?"

"Two blocks over. Best one I've ever eaten at."

"I'll get my coat and meet you by the elevator in five."

CHLOE WATCHED him walk out of her office. Still, he wasn't bad to look at.

She closed her laptop and shoved the notes she'd taken into her drawer haphazardly. Maybe the day wouldn't have been so bad if she'd done like Jody had suggested and gone out of the office. But wasn't she mad at Jason too?

No. That was the problem. As much as she wanted to hate him for taking her job, she was finding it hard to actually not like him.

She'd hit him in the head with a stapler, causing him to get stitches, and still he was kind to her.

Maybe it was time for a change. She thought about Melanie Peet's little gift shop in Aubrey Heights and how excited she was to show Chloe around. And what about that quaint coffee shop that had opened up? Christmas was magical there.

Christmas.

She'd nearly forgotten that the holidays were upon them. She was so focused on not getting her promotion and the potential of losing the contract with *Pop! Cosmetics* that she decided she'd become quite a Scrooge.

Jason appeared in her door again. This time with his wool coat, scarf, and leather gloves. Wasn't he a picture?

"Are you ready?" he asked, his body illuminated from behind by a security light. The sharp lines of his face were accentuated, and his eyes even darker as he narrowed them on her.

"Yeah, I think I am," she said aloud to him as much as she said it to herself. Seeing him there, wanting to hate him, but also finding herself pulled toward attraction, she decided she was indeed ready—for a change.

JASON COULD FEEL her fuming as they walked silently in the bitter cold toward the deli she'd told him about. There was a storm brewing, one that was promising at least four inches of snow, and of course, bitter cold.

"Are you okay? I swear you're growling," Chloe asked as she opened the door of the deli.

He was going to be honest with her. For some reason he felt as if she needed that from him. "Just was thinking about Deborah."

"No, put the bite in it. *Deb*. It makes it more sinister, especially since you're growling."

Jason chuckled. He pondered Chloe Richardson as she moved to the counter and ordered a corned beef sandwich, half of it for now, and the other half wrapped to take with her.

What was her story? City girl from birth? Small town transplant? He couldn't actually figure it out, except that he knew, what he assumed was home, was hours away. Another city? Something more quaint?

She'd gathered her order and paid, though he'd meant to, but he was more caught up in watching her. She took extra condiments and only filled her fountain drink a quarter of the way with ice. She was frugal, wanting to get the most out of everything she could.

Jason placed his order and picked it up at the end of the counter, aware that Chloe had gone to sit down and begin her meal. Was she that put off by him? Perhaps she was just hungry.

Sitting across from her, Jason placed his napkin on his lap. "Corned beef, huh?"

"A favorite. My dad used to get them when he'd come to the city, and he'd bring half back for me."

Childhood memory, he'd take that little nugget. "Come to the city, so where is home if not in the city?"

Her eyes were cautiously on his as she took a bite

of her sandwich before setting it on the paper and chewing. "Aubrey Heights."

He had to think quickly, but it came to him. "They have a whole Christmas motif."

"Yes," she said but her eyes still held the same caution. "You've been there?"

"Yeah, lots of times. My mother was fanatical about the candle shop they have there."

A smile formed on Chloe's lips, which also had mustard smeared on them. God if she wasn't the most adorable woman he'd ever seen.

"Abby Foster has owned that store since I was a little girl. In elementary school we would take field trips to her store and she'd let us dip our own candles. My mother has a collection of Chloe's finest."

Her skin pinked when she talked of home, and there was a shimmer in her eyes.

"I remember the chocolate store," he sat back in his chair and crossed his legs, suddenly not hungry but ecstatic that he could watch the change in her expression each time he brought up something new.

"The Adlers own that. I have to stay away from their store though. It's so good I make myself sick," she said on a laugh before she took another bite. "When were you there last?"

Jason thought about it. "The Christmas before my mom moved to Florida. So five years now?" He remembered because it was after that his father had died.

"Did you just visit for a day, or did you make a vacation of it?"

"My mother did like to stay at the little inn on the edge of town. But the past few times were only day trips."

Her shoulders had eased, and she played with the straw in her cup, which he found sweet as she was occupied with her thoughts. "It's covered in snow right now," she said looking off into the distance. "Carriage rides were just beginning. The roasted chestnut vendors will have carts out this week. The carolers will start singing every night. Oh, and the tree will be lit on the first." She sighed, and Jason wasn't sure she even knew she'd taken a trip in her head.

"I'd love to see it. Especially covered in snow."

"Magical," she contemplated. Then as if she realized she'd become all dreamy about what she'd given up back home, she straightened and took another bite of her sandwich. "Where are you from?"

"Here."

"Here? That's it?"

"What more is there? Raised in an apartment, and then a town house. No backyard swing sets for me. I always had a park nearby."

"As an adult, I love city-living. I can't even imagine it as a kid."

"It wasn't so bad," he proposed. But then again a yard would have been magical.

"So, tell me what you know about *Deb*."

CHAPTER 10

*W*as he squirming in his seat? Chloe put down her sandwich and watched as he tore the paper from his straw and jabbed it into his drink.

Deborah King was a bigger deal than just some ad exec who swooped in and threatened to take the deal away from Chloe. The very mention of her name had Jason's expression going from humored, asking her questions, to nearly fearful as if he were under interrogation.

He took the top piece of bread off his sandwich, pulled off the tomato, and discarded it. Chloe noticed his hands shook. She'd certainly gone into some kind of territory with him on this, though the whole point of letting him take her to dinner, which she realized she'd paid for, was so that they could talk about *Deb*.

After a few moments, she wondered if he'd forgotten she'd asked him a question, but finally he looked up at her.

"Deborah King," he began and then let out a long, slow breath. "She's the reason I left *Stockton*."

"Oh," Chloe sighed. "Did she swoop in and take

your position?" She hadn't meant for the bite of the words to be so sharp, but they were.

He shook his head as if it hadn't meant anything, or he hadn't noticed the tone. "I worked with her for five years. She's great at what she does. She can land any account she goes after, and she delivers. The woman is a workhorse."

"And she didn't leave any business for you?" The bite was still there, and Chloe assumed it would be for a while. After all, deep inside she was still trying hard not to like Jason Mitchell.

"She shared. My client list was impressive."

"Why leave?"

Chloe could see the red settle in his cheeks. Anger? Embarrassment? "Sexual harassment in the work place isn't always dished out by men."

That had Chloe easing back in the booth. "Oh." What else could she say?

"Two years into our working relationship, I thought she was a tough gal, but she seemed to like me just fine. We worked okay together and she was teaching me a lot. Then it became lunches out and we'd go meet clients together. She had a flat tire and I drove her home once, and she asked me in, but I didn't go in. Of course, somewhere she'd prefaced that with the fact her husband was out of town on business, but I didn't pay much attention to that. The little things began to build into big things and I'll admit, I got a little confused. She's ten years my senior, and she was looking at me as if she were hungry for me."

Jason stopped, picked up his drink, and sipped before continuing.

"I caved a little. Just a little," he emphasized as he lifted his head and looked Chloe straight in the eye. "It was one night in the elevator when I was leaving late. The doors were closing and she ran toward it waving her hands. I held it open and she slid in. A few floors down and she pushed the button to stop the car."

He took another sip of his drink and cleared his throat. "I knew what was going to happen and I let it. She moved in and kissed me. A hot and heavy kiss that had me backing to the wall. Her hands were in my hair, under my shirt, and down..." He didn't continue with the details. "Anyway, something happened after we were done groping each other in the elevator. We got downstairs and someone was there who needed her to go back up with them. Account crisis and all. There were a few more of those incidents, and I knew people were catching on. Then at the Christmas party I met her husband, and it all hit me that this was a serious thing that was happening. This woman was slapping my ass in passing. Groping me in the break room, and texting me at all times of the night."

He pushed away his sandwich and shook his head. "I'm not a home wrecker. I'm not someone's play toy. I take relationships seriously, and I won't be with a woman who doesn't take them seriously too. So, I stopped playing her games."

"And then she went after you?"

He lifted his head, and clarity shimmered from his eyes. "You could say that. Suddenly my accounts started to disappear. Connections I had no longer wanted to talk to me. She'd make her moves and I'd deny her, and then I'd get written up over something foolish. I dealt with it for a long time before I met William and he offered me the job."

Her job, Chloe thought. But for some reason, this time when it crossed her mind it didn't anger her as it might have before. This time she just felt sorry for him.

"That's horrible. Did you turn her in?"

"To where? If I filed charges against her she'd come back at me with *he was involved too* or turn it around on me."

"She'd be the victim?"

"Yeah. So it was easier to start over."

Chloe wrapped up the half of the sandwich she'd been eating. Suddenly she wasn't so hungry anymore. She'd never even considered that sexual harassment could go both ways, which was horribly naive of her.

It also had put some of her emotions in check when it came to Jason. She'd been mad from the moment she'd learned that he was there for the position she'd wanted. But then she did like to watch him walk out of a room. Was she equally as horrible as *Deb*?

No, she wasn't in the same boat as someone who sexually harassed, but she was abusive. Dear God! The stitches on his head were because of her. She could feel the warmth of irritation begin under her suit coat.

"It just pisses me off that she's still chasing my clients—the firm's clients," he corrected. "You worked your ass off for that account, there is no way in hell I'm going to let Deborah King walk in and take it away from you."

She felt her mouth fall open. He would fight for her? Why? She'd been nothing but a bitch to him from the moment he'd walked into her office. "It's not up to us if Gloria signs with us or not. I've done all the foot work and they know what I have to offer."

Jason slowly nodded. "Let's go back and I'll look over the contract you gave to Gloria. Maybe we can come up with some extra incentives that you can offer. Let's be in the lobby of *Pop! Cosmetics* first thing in the morning and we can present them to her. She will want to work with us. You deserve this account."

Something happened in that moment that Chloe couldn't quite explain. This man that had wrecked her world four days ago, whom she'd assaulted with a stapler, still wanted what was best for her. If it wasn't inappropriate, especially considering the topic of conversation about *Deb*, she would jump across the table and kiss the man on the mouth. Instead she stared at him formulating her two word reply. "Thank you."

"Let's take this back to the office. Are you good to keep working for a bit?" He looked at his watch. "It's nearly seven-thirty."

"I'm fine. Long hours don't bother me."

"Do you need to go home and change or any-thing? Not that you don't look nice in your suit, I just thought..."

"I have gym clothes in my office. You're right. It would be nice to be comfortable."

Jason laughed. "I have gym clothes in my office too. We'll take our dinner back and get to work."

CHAPTER 11

They'd gone back to the office and in different directions without another word. Chloe knew Jason's mind was spinning out new ideas. She'd seen that look a million times in the mirror.

Perhaps they were more alike than she'd like to admit.

As she wiggled her toes, which were covered in her favorite workout socks, she wondered how important *Pop! Cosmetics* really was to the company. If they lost it, would it really matter? They had plenty of business. Yes, this would be one of the biggest accounts ever landed for the firm, but did it make or break anything?

By Friday, she could have three more smaller accounts brought in and under contract. Why had it been so important to have this one? It hadn't done her any favors. In fact, she'd spent so much time courting Gloria Vandenberg, she'd lost her promotion.

Jason turned into her office, a pair of sweatpants, NYU T-shirt, and bare feet. There was a zing of remorse for looking at him the way she had. It seemed so intimate to see him barefooted, as if they were having a sleepover in her office.

She shook the thought from her head. There wouldn't be a moment where she looked at him and didn't think about Deborah King looking at him the same way. He was a professional. He'd gone into the office to work on a Sunday, and she'd thrown a stapler at his head. He'd stayed late to help her land the biggest client of her career, and she was sizing him up.

"Gloria Vandenberg is one loaded young lady," he said as he flipped through papers he carried in with him. "Do you know what she's worth?"

"Of course," Chloe said with a nod. "She's very talented too. She has an eye for color and fashion."

"Yeah, she does. She's a social media genius too. I mean, it doesn't hurt to have some of the influential friends she has either."

"They've done a lot for her," she agreed. "What are you getting at?"

He walked to her desk and sat down in the chair that faced her. "Why does she even want to use a company to promote her? I mean, seriously. In the day and age of social media, and the influencer market she's got, does she need us?"

Chloe was sure her mouth had fallen open. Was he serious?

"If she's a savvy business woman, just as she is, she knows there is more than social media. She needs us for the greater picture. Social media doesn't do TV commercials, radio spots, magazine ads, billboards, and…"

"I get it." He flipped through the printed pages he'd brought in. "What angle are you going with on this?"

"The angle I'm going with, is that we need to get

these new options you talked about to her as soon as possible, and then decide on the angle."

"Right, but Deborah is going to come in with guns blazing. She knows as much as we do about the amount of money this girl has. We need to offer some big options for her."

"You want me to re-pitch to her?"

Jason leaned in, his arms rested on her desk. "Yes. I want you to re-pitch to her. Let's hit her in the heart. She had a sister die of cancer at the age of six."

"How do you know that?"

"How do you not?" he asked as he leaned back in his seat. "That's the kind of stuff you dig for."

"And you want me to walk in and say, *Hey, I know your sister died as a child and you should sign with me?*"

The smile that turned up the corners of his mouth lit in his eyes. "She can do some good for the world with this company she's started. What if we have her consider a line that will benefit childhood cancer? Special colors. Special packaging. An ad campaign where she can open up about her sister."

And this was why the man had taken her job. He was brilliant.

"A personal angle on a bigger picture."

His eyes creased as his smile grew wider. "Exactly. Why have something this big without helping the world, right?"

"Right," she agreed, her voice airy. "Here is the contract that I gave her."

Chloe slid the papers across the desk to him and watched as he began to read each page. By the second page he had reached for her pen and began to make notes.

Two cups of coffee, a walk to the bathroom, and a trip to the vending machine later, Jason set the well-noted contract back on her desk.

"These are my suggestions to amending the contract. I think you'll find that she will jump at these new opportunities."

Chloe flipped through the pages. Nearly every clause, every exception, every promise was noted. She wanted to throw the papers back at him, but she found that every note he'd added was genius.

"I'll get this written up," Chloe said, lifting her eyes to his.

Jason smiled. "Are you sure you're up for it?" He looked at his watch, which she noticed was a Rolex. "It's ten o'clock."

"And we're going to be sitting in her office when she walks in," Chloe promised. "Let me get to work on this. If you want to go home…"

"We're in this together. I'm here until we're done."

The smile he kept steady on her twisted in her stomach. Was Deborah King drawn in by him like this? Were her actions as vicious as he'd made them out to be? Why did she want to jump across that desk and kiss him, just as she'd wanted to in the restaurant? It was ridiculous.

"I'm going to get some water from the break room. I'll bring you one. I think you've had enough coffee."

Chloe looked at her shaking hand and laughed. "I guess I have."

Taking the papers from her desk, she turned toward her computer screen and began making the amendments to the contract they would offer to Gloria Vandenberg in the morning.

JASON WALKED to the break room, filled with the glow of the city lights outside. He opened the refrigerator and pulled out two bottles of water. As he closed the refrigerator, he leaned up against it to gather himself.

Sitting in Chloe's office for the past three hours, he'd had a lot of time to watch her work, and gaze at her. The moment she'd pulled her dark hair up into a ponytail, his breath had caught in his chest. Her slender neck was exposed. Immediately his mind had gone to the thought of grazing his lips over the delicate skin. He'd had to excuse himself and take a walk around the office.

There was no way he could act on the thoughts that were rolling in his head. At dinner he'd told her about Deborah King and the advances she'd made on him. How could he possibly consider the things he'd been thinking about Chloe? Besides, he'd sworn he'd never get involved with someone in the office again. The cost was too great.

Taking in a few more deep breaths, he started back to Chloe's office.

She sat facing her computer. Her fingers moved over the keys of her keyboard swiftly. A pencil was now tucked behind her ear, and her last cup of coffee had been pushed to the side.

A small diamond stud sparkled from her earlobe in the light of the desk lamp. Were they a gift? Had she purchased them herself? He found that he desperately wanted to touch them.

Swallowing hard he squeezed the bottle in his hand.

"Here," he said as he set the bottle on her desk. "How's it coming?"

"Good. I have ten pages left to go. My eyes are blurring though. We don't have time to proofread this thing before we take it in."

He hadn't thought about that. "We'll get it done, then come back early and go over it."

She shifted a look up at him. "We're going to look like a pair of zombies walking in tomorrow."

"Wouldn't be the first time for me," he admitted.

"Me either." She smiled before she turned back and continued her work at her computer.

CHAPTER 12

*A*s she turned off the lamp on her desk, Chloe yawned. The clock on her desk said it was eleven-thirty.

She rubbed her eyes and pushed back her aching shoulders. Tilting her head from side to side, she wondered how they were going to pull this off.

Jason stood in the doorway of her office, his gym bag in his hand and his messenger bag on his shoulder. "Ready?"

"Yeah."

"Do you have your car here?"

Chloe shook her head. "No. I'm only about twelve blocks from here."

"It's the middle of the night. I'd feel better if you didn't walk home tonight."

She shrugged. "I've done it before."

"I could get us a cab," he offered.

Chloe considered his offer. It was cold outside. She'd made the walk many times, but she had to admit that it did frighten her on occasion.

"I'll pay for half."

She watched as he took a breath as if to argue, but

didn't. Instead he gave her a nod and waited for her to gather her things and together they walked to the elevator.

The floor was dark, but for the glow from the emergency lights. When the elevator arrived and the doors opened it flooded them with light. Chloe blinked against them as Jason waited for her to enter before he did.

He pressed the button for the ground floor and they rode in silence.

There was something about the sight of him in his gym clothes, his wool coat, and messenger bag covering him from the impending cold. His cologne was faint, but she could still smell it floating on the stale air of the elevator.

Her mind raced with the information he'd given her about Deborah King's moves in the elevator. The thought of her moving in and kissing him, touching him, taking him, had Chloe's breath hitch and her head spin. Lifting her eyes to watch him, she wondered what was going through his head. Did he think of that moment too?

She needed to push the thought of him out of her head. That morning she'd despised him. Standing there wondering if he'd react to her if she moved in and kissed him in the elevator was asinine.

He'd taken her job. He'd kept her at the office until nearly midnight. She was working harder than she'd ever worked, and was it because Deborah King was moving in on her client? Why would she have done that if not to be taking swipes at Jason?

"You doing okay? You look tired," Jason's voice broke her from thought as the doors opened.

"Yeah. Yeah, I'm fine."

"Let's meet back here at seven. We'll go over the contract and we can be to *Pop! Cosmetics* by eight."

"Sure."

A faint smile formed on his lips, but his eyes shadowed with concern. "I have a cab out front."

"Thank you," she said, lowering her gaze from his, and walked out into the lobby of the building.

As he'd said, the cab waited just outside the door. Jason opened the door for her and she slid across the seat as he climbed in. She gave her address to the driver and they pulled away from the building.

The city had a fresh blanket of snow since they'd walked to the deli hours earlier. It sparkled in the streetlamp lights, and she thought it looked magnificently romantic.

"Thank you for all the work you put in tonight," Jason said, and she turned to see him smiling at her. "You're going to land this. I have no doubt."

But the compliment pierced her. Now it wasn't her that was landing the account. It was them. They were a team—perhaps a bit unwillingly. Did he feel as if he had to swoop in and save the account for them? Was he feeling guilty that they were even in the position they were in?

The cab pulled up in front of her building, and Chloe gathered her things and opened the door.

As she stepped out, Jason slid across the seat to where she'd been and climbed out. Chloe gripped her bag a little tighter. She wasn't going to let him walk her inside, she thought as he closed the door to the cab.

"I'll watch to make sure you get in safe. My mother always taught me to do so." He smiled and it caused her stomach to knot. "Get some sleep," he said, standing next to the cab. "I can't wait to see Deborah King's face when she loses this account."

And right there everything Chloe had been considering rushed through her head.

"Is that why you're so focused on landing this account?" Chloe asked as the snow increased around them. "You want this account so you can stick it to Deborah King?"

"What? No. It's a bonus, but no."

"Are you sure? It seems like you have a vendetta against her and this would be icing on the cake."

"Sure it would."

"So you've made it your project?"

He stepped away from the cab and reached his hand out touching Chloe's arm. "This is your account. You've done all the work, you deserve..."

"It was my account. I worked my ass off to get it, and then you show up and it all goes to hell. Why is that? How did you manage to come along just as I was working on this? Did William think I couldn't handle it? Did he know you'd do anything to take it over from *Deb*?"

"Chloe, what is this all about? We're a team."

"No. I was flying solo and doing a damn good job of it until you walked into the office."

Her words hurt, and she could see the result of them in his expression. As he frowned down at her, he touched his stitches, which were now getting wet in the snow.

"You were doing a great job. You do a great job. I didn't mean to step on your toes. I was only trying to help."

"Great. Your help was Deborah King moving in on my client."

He opened his mouth and shut it again. "I think we both need some sleep. I'll see you in the morning."

Jason turned and slid back into the cab, but the car didn't drive away. A moment later he rolled down his window. "Go inside. You're getting wet out here. So go."

Out of spite she could have stood on that street until the sun came up, but she didn't. She turned and let herself inside of the building, then watched as the cab pulled away from the curb.

CHAPTER 13

*W*hat had he truly expected from her? Jason's intentions were nothing but helpful. He had half a mind to have the driver turn back around and he'd knock on her door and tell her as much.

No, he understood where she was coming from. She was threatened by his very presence, and hadn't he felt that way himself when Deborah began to take his accounts from him when she didn't get what she wanted?

He wanted her to land the account as much for Chloe as he wanted to make sure Deborah King didn't. How could he prove to her that he wanted the best for her? He wanted the best for the firm. He wanted the best for himself, and that shouldn't feel as dirty as it did.

Jason liked Chloe, and the cutthroat industry they were in didn't give much leeway for understanding. Everyone was out to make it themselves and break the competition. He'd thrived on that most of his adult life.

When the driver stopped in front of his building, he paid the fare and climbed out. As the cab disappeared into the curtain of snow, he wondered what the next morning would entail. Could Chloe put her differences aside for a few hours? There was no doubt in his mind that she could manage the account on her own, but he wanted to be there to represent the firm. It was a package deal. Chloe, even if she landed the account on her own, would always have a team behind her to help her. He was part of that team.

Damn her. He wasn't going to give up on this and it didn't have anything to do with Deborah King, though he would like to see her bite it. Chloe Richardson deserved the *Pop! Cosmetics* account, and he was going to see that she got it.

JASON UNLOCKED his office door at six-thirty the next morning. Streetlights still glowed and the snow beneath them shimmered as he looked out over the wakening city.

The office was quiet, and he preferred it that way.

Jason hung up his coat and headed to the break room to make a cup of coffee. By six-forty-five he was seated in Chloe's office, sipping on his coffee, waiting for her to arrive. When he heard the bell chime from the church down the street, he realized seven o'clock was upon them. The office had begun to stir, but Chloe hadn't walked through the door yet.

After fifteen more minutes, he walked to the break room and filled his cup of coffee again. They'd had an agreement. They'd meet at seven and go over the contract again. Where was she?

When she hadn't arrived by seven-forty-five he looked up her phone number and called.

"Where are you?" he began the moment he heard her weary voice on the other end.

"I'm sitting in Gloria Vandenberg's office waiting for her to arrive."

"You're what?" He walked swiftly to his office and yanked his coat from the rack. "I thought we were going to proof the changes to the contract before we went over together."

"I decided that I could proof it myself, and this is my client. I can handle this."

Jason gripped his phone tightly in his hand as he hurried to the elevator. "We're a team, Chloe. Why are you doing this?"

"Because I can do this on my own. I landed the client to begin with. I can finish the deal," her voice screeched through the phone as the doors to the elevator closed. "I don't need your supervision."

"My super—" he gritted his teeth as the elevator opened to the lobby. That was the last straw. Let her fail, he thought. He had his job. Why he was so worried about her feelings and her successes didn't even make sense to him. "I look forward to hearing about your meeting," he offered as he pressed the button to take him back up to his office.

* * *

CHLOE TUCKED her phone back into her bag, after having silenced it. The last thing she needed was to have her meeting with Gloria Vandenberg interrupted.

She heard the distinct sound of Gloria's laugh a moment before she opened the inner door to her office and walked through it. Chloe stood as Gloria, in yoga attire and her mass of dark curls piled high on her head, walked in with another woman also in yoga attire.

"Chloe, I'm so glad to see you. We just did hot

yoga and it was invigorating," Gloria took the towel from her shoulder and wiped her face. Walking to the small refrigerator behind her desk, she took out a bottle of water for herself and one for the woman who had walked in with her. "Can I get you something, Chloe?"

"I'm fine. Thank you."

Gloria opened the water and took a long drink, all the while the woman with her, her blonde hair pulled in a bun, watched Chloe carefully.

"So, what do you have for me?" Gloria asked as she sat down behind her desk.

Chloe exchanged looks with the woman and then with Gloria, who didn't seem to have any thoughts about excusing the woman.

She pulled the contract from her bag. "I've got some changes to the contract for you to look over. We've added some new options for you to consider."

"Great." Gloria sat forward to take the contract from her. Immediately she began to skim through it, flipping pages, and then going back. "You've been doing a lot of thinking on this."

"Yes. We think we'd be a good fit, and we'd have a dedicated team for your account," she confided in her as the woman continued to watch her.

"I like that." Gloria continued to look at the contract. "You know legal should look at this."

"Of course. I wouldn't dream of it not going through the right channels."

"I have the other contract to consider as well," Gloria noted with a quick glance at the woman who stood between them, a crease now defined between her brows.

"I understand."

Gloria continued to look at the contract and the corner of her mouth lifted. "You know, there is just something about this contract that feels right. You and I have been working together for a bit now on this, and I wouldn't feel right if you weren't working on this."

Gloria took a pink pen from the top drawer of her desk and held it in her fingers over the contract before looking up at the woman that stood to her side. "Why don't we catch up later," she said to the woman whose cheeks had become red. "We can do more yoga next week."

"Gloria, I think you need to have legal look at that before you sign it. You have a lot at stake, I'm sure you don't need to be reminded of that," the woman argued.

"I know. Oh, I didn't introduce the two of you. Chloe Richardson this is Deb," Gloria offered non-chalantly.

Chloe felt the blood drain from her head. "Deborah King?" With her hair piled on her head and her skin bright red from the yoga, she didn't look anything like her professional photos online.

Deb's eyes narrowed on her. "How do you know who I am?"

"I know."

Deborah's lips pursed. "*Mason Arts*, right? You're their glory girl?"

Glory girl? Oh, Chloe liked the sound of that. "I'm with *Mason Arts*, yes."

"Too small to take care of *Pop! Cosmetics*. No matter who they've put in charge."

Gloria lifted her head. "Who did they put in charge?"

Deborah shook her head. "No one important." She turned her attention to Gloria. "I think it would be best if you ran that contract through legal," she reiterated the need for her to not sign it.

"I ran yours through legal. I've run four others through legal," she said, and Chloe tried her hardest to not let the shock resonate on her face. She'd thought she'd had the account in the bag. She'd had no idea anyone else was in the running until *Deb* had come along. Gloria lifted her strong chin and smiled in Chloe's direction. "Chloe has sass, smarts, and a fire that I admire. Her firm is small, but I like that. I like that they're willing to reach out to a company as big as mine. It's not going to be easy, and they're going to fail on some of this," she noted as she tapped her pink pen to her cheek. "But she's going to work her ass off to keep me happy."

"*Stockton* will do the same," Deborah pointed out.

"I'm sure they will." Gloria smiled again at Chloe and signed her name to the contract. "Chloe, honey, I look forward to doing business with you."

Chloe stood and took a breath to thank her, but Deborah moved in and placed her hands on Gloria's desk. "Are you kidding me? You signed that? Are you stupid?"

"Oh, I'm not stupid. Never stupid."

"We've spent nearly the entire week together. We just did yoga together for Christ sake."

"Yes, and if you'd like to do it again next week, I'm game."

"Why would I want to do that?"

Gloria eased back in her chair, a smile radiating from her lips. "Deb, business and friendship are two different things. I can be your friend and not want to do business with you because I don't believe in your ethics. I can be your friend, but not like how you slapped my assistant's ass as we walked through design two days ago. I can be your friend and want to do yoga, lunch, drinks, you name it, but not like that you proposed a two man team and they have eight."

Deborah eased up, her lips tight. "You've made a great mistake. Your company will pay for it. I hope you understand what you've done. You're young and naive."

"I think I've done what is right here. Perhaps we can't be friends if you can't understand how I do business."

Deborah turned to Chloe. "Tell him he didn't win this. If that was his motive in adding such features to the contract."

"I'm sure I don't know what you're talking about," Chloe offered, keeping her voice steady. "I'm going to take very good care of Miss Vandenberg."

Gloria picked up her phone and pressed a button. "Jeffery, Ms. King is ready to go. Can you have her car pulled up to the front and her things gathered from the other room, please?"

Deborah pushed her shoulders back and walked to the door. "This isn't the last you'll hear from me," she promised as she opened the door and slammed it behind her.

Gloria laughed before she stood and extended a hand to Chloe. "I look forward to doing business with you," Chloe beamed.

"Likewise."

"And I didn't mean to come between you and Deborah. I didn't think you'd sign this without having it looked over."

Gloria shrugged. "Honey, I've never played by the rules. Go read some tabloids. I like you. I like what you have to offer. I know there are going to be obstacles because this is bigger than your firm. But you have balls if you want to swim in the same ocean with us. I want to see you succeed."

And that was why Chloe had been drawn to Gloria Vandenberg.

CHAPTER 14

The sleeves of his dress shirt had been rolled up and his tie had been loosened. The cup of coffee on his desk had gone cold and his temper had gone hot.

Jason paced behind his desk, in front of the bank of windows that looked out over the busy city. All the people below him went about their day without knowing that he was stewing in his office over Chloe's insubordination.

He had the power to fire her. The thought had crossed his mind. So had the thought of kissing her in the elevator the night before, but that was totally irrelevant. He worked with the woman and that was rule number one in his book—never date a co-worker or be involved in any way—and maybe that was just his bullshit way of talking himself out of something good.

Deciding to get some work done, and forget about the *Pop! Cosmetics* account, Jason turned to sit at his desk when he saw Chloe headed toward him.

The scarf was still tied around her neck and her coat was buttoned with fresh snow on her shoulder.

The woman had on a skirt and stilettos. She was crazy, he decided. Who wore that stuff in the snow?

There was a power that resonated from her as she walked right through the door and threw a manila envelope on his desk.

"Read it and weep," she said as she plopped down in the chair in front of his desk and crossed her legs.

"What is this?" he asked, making sure to not look at her legs.

"Open it."

He didn't like her game. For all he knew, it could be her resignation. After all, she must not have thought enough of him to have waited for him as they had arranged.

Jason picked up the envelope and opened it. Pulling out the contents he looked up at her. "This is the contract for *Pop! Cosmetics.*"

"Sure as hell is. Flip to the back page," she said smugly.

Jason did just that and his breath caught in his lungs. "She signed this."

"Oh, baby, not only did she sign it without taking it to legal first, she signed it in front of *Deb*," she exclaimed as she stood from her chair and sat on the edge of his desk.

"You're kidding me?"

"I couldn't even make that up."

"Why? Why was *Deb*—Deborah there?"

Chloe shrugged. "They did hot yoga. But she liked our proposal better."

"Oh, my God."

"Oh, my God!" Chloe echoed his cheer. "We got it."

Jason walked around to the front of his desk and pulled her up and into a tight embrace. "You got it. You did this," he said as he hugged her so tightly he could have broken her.

"We," she reiterated, her breath warm in his ear, before she eased back to look at him. "A lot of what won her over were the additions you made. The exclusive team spoke to her."

"I knew it would," he agreed as he looked at her, still wrapped in his arms.

This should have been the moment he let her go and took a step back, but he couldn't seem to release her. His theory of not falling for co-workers was just that, bullshit. Those blue eyes which contrasted with her dark hair stunned him into paralysis. He could hold her right there for the rest of the day. He wanted to hold her right there.

Chloe managed to push back from him and take those necessary steps to distance them, perhaps she could read the internal conflict in his eyes. "We need to set up a meeting with the people we want on the *Pop! Cosmetics* team. We need to make some plans as to what we want to do first. We need to get Gloria's budget in place. We need a meeting with Gloria and her team."

She was pacing now and he watched as the genius he'd only heard about began to work.

"Whatever you need, you just let me know. I'll make sure we have the people to make this work. You know the staff better than I do. Tell me who you want to work with, and I'll make sure they're covered on their other projects."

Chloe lifted her head and smiled at him. "Thank you. I was sure you were here to steal this away from me."

"I would never do that to you."

"I believe you now. I'm sorry I didn't wait for you this morning."

"I guess you knew what you were doing."

"I'll get to work on this. I should have a basic outline of a plan by the end of the day." She started for the door.

"Chloe," he called to her and she turned to him. "Congratulations. You deserve this."

"Thank you."

CHLOE MANAGED her way around the corner before she took a breath. She'd done it, and he was happy for her. They got the account—she got the account. *Pop! Cosmetics* was hers to run. Who needed the management position? She'd gotten what she'd wanted.

When she turned into her office, she gently shut the door before she leaned against it and pressed her hand to her chest. The contract, the jab at *Deb*, the thought of running an entire team for one account was somehow diminished by Jason holding her against him in his office. Had he even realized what that had done to her?

It was innocent. He'd hugged her to congratulate her on a job well done, but it had lingered. There was no way he would have considered that it was more than that, not in light of what he'd told her about Deborah King doing the same thing to him. It was a friendly gesture, but oh how it shook her to her toes.

Even now she could hardly balance on the stilettos she'd chosen to wear in the snow just to impress Gloria.

The very thought of Deborah King's expression made the moment that Gloria signed that contract even sweeter.

Chloe moved her hand from her racing heart to her fluttering stomach.

She had to let those impulsive feelings of attraction go. She couldn't even consider Jason as anything other than her boss—but, oh, that embrace.

Slowly she walked to her desk and sat down. There was a lot to do, and for the next few weeks they would be short staffed. The holidays always seemed to have people flying here and there, and their heads certainly weren't in work mode—and neither was she.

The discussion she and Jason had had last night about Aubrey Heights took her away to the snow-packed streets, carolers, sleigh rides, and quaint storefronts. And he'd been there—Jason had felt its magic.

Would he like to go again? Would it be too personal for him to see the town through her eyes? It would be a celebration of sorts. They were a good team.

What would her mother think?

She shook her head. God, she was a mess. What would her mother think if she took Jason home? She'd think they were an item, and they were the furthest thing from it.

Chloe Richardson had just landed the biggest account of her career, and she'd slyly done it behind Jason Mitchell's back. That wasn't something that started a good relationship anyway. Besides, they weren't going there, and her emotions were just stirred anyway because of the holidays and not getting the job she'd thought she'd wanted.

What she really wanted was to make Gloria Vandenberg happy, and she was going to put everything into making sure that happened.

Chloe opened her notebook to a fresh page and picked up her pen. It was time to get her head out of the fluffy snow clouds and back to the task at hand.

CHAPTER 15

*A*s much as he wanted to sit at Chloe's desk and watch her mind work, Jason kept his distance. He'd taken six calls from clients who had heard he'd left *Stockton* and wanted to move their accounts to *Mason Arts*. It seemed as if Deborah was making the wrong kind of splash, and he couldn't help but find humor in her misfortune.

Oh, what he would have given to have seen her face when Gloria Vandenberg signed the contract for Chloe. He wasn't one to wish anything bad on anyone, but there seemed to be some justice in it happening.

He'd hoped to have seen her plan before lunch, and it would have given him a reason to offer to take her out. Just a business lunch. A celebration lunch. A working lunch. But Chloe had yet to emerge from her office.

When he finally decided he'd order in deli, and he'd get some for her too, William knocked on his door and let himself in.

"My dad says you've had a busy day." The grin on William's face was as phony as the Rolex on his wrist. He made himself at home in one of the chairs that faced Jason, and kicked his feet up on the desk. "I knew bringing you on was going to be a stellar idea."

"I appreciate that. But the biggest news of the day is Chloe bringing in *Pop! Cosmetics.*"

William shrugged and adjusted his watch. "That should have been finalized last week."

"I think it worked out for the best," Jason primed. "The contract has more built in, and it'll bring in more revenue."

"It needs more people to work it."

"It's a big account."

"You'll be overseeing, so it's in good hands." William dropped his feet to the floor. "Got a lunch date. Why don't we plan to meet at six for drinks? I want to go over your objectives with *Pop!*"

"Chloe is making the plan now. I can bring her along."

William shook his head. "Just you. You're in charge." He pointed his fingers at Jason in the shape of a gun and gave him a wink as he walked back out the door.

Jason eased back in his seat. Byron Mason was a much different man than his son. William had that spoiled-in-charge attitude that made Jason sick. It had been a turn off to working for the company, initially, but the need to get out of *Stockton* was great, and Byron had won him over in the end. He was a good man with a good business sense. It wasn't the first time that Jason had worked for a company with a self-centered boss' kid as his boss. In life, he'd found that those who were raised by the boss usually worked harder than anyone for less acclaim, but there were a few that gave that position a bad name.

Deciding to order in that lunch, Jason turned to his computer and saw Chloe emerge for the first time since he'd talked to her that morning. She stopped by Jody's desk—he was certain of the woman's name now—and then headed to the elevator with her coat on and the scarf tied around her neck again.

Maybe if he hurried he could cash in on getting her to have lunch with him.

Nearly taking the corner of his desk into his thigh, he headed for the door. Grabbing his coat off the rack, he hurried to the elevator, just as Chloe stepped in.

"Hold that for me?" He called out and saw her hand slide between the doors. "Thanks."

"Rushing out?" she asked as she pulled her gloves from her pocket and slid them on her dainty hands.

"Need to get some lunch. Are you going to walk far in those shoes?" he asked looking down at her feet.

"I'm a master in high heels," she humored. "I have a cab waiting for me. I won't be in the elements long."

"Oh, you're heading out?"

"Tyler Ashby asked me to meet him for lunch."

Jason thought on the name. It was familiar, but he couldn't piece it together. "Who is Tyler Ashby?"

"*Needed Bean Coffee*. There are eight of them in a ten mile radius of our building and sixty more throughout the state."

"No kidding? He's one of our clients, right?"

When she smiled it radiated. "It was one of the first clients I brought in during my internship. I went to college with Tyler. We dated actually. He inherited the first store from his father who was big into sourcing beans from economies that needed an income boost. Tyler was a genius and turned it into what it is today."

For some reason Jason got stuck on the *dated* part of the conversation. "So this is a business meeting?"

"Lunch with a client who is a friend. We were going to go out for dinner, but this worked better."

Dinner meant date, didn't it? he thought as the elevator door opened.

"I'll see you in a bit. I promise not to be gone too long," Chloe called back to him as she pulled up the collar of her coat and walked out into the snow toward the cab that waited for her.

Jason watched her disappear and his heart sank. This was asinine. Why did he care that she was having lunch with Tyler Ashby? He was bringing money into the firm that paid Jason's bills. It was a good thing that she had a good relationship with the man. And if she was dating him, it was none of Jason's business.

His stomach growled and he figured he'd better make the most of his run down to the street. Outside there was a hotdog vendor braving the cold to bring the masses of the city a mediocre meal. Who was he to pass that up?

CHLOE SAT BACK in the cab as it maneuvered through lunchtime city traffic. If she hadn't known better, she would have thought that Jason had run to the elevator just to talk to her.

Wasn't that a stupid thought? Well, not really, she reconsidered. She was working on the biggest deal the firm had ever landed. He was going to want to know her every move until the team was working like a well-oiled machine. Gloria would appreciate that too. She had also been on Chloe's phone multiple times that morning to check in.

Lunch with Tyler would be the icing on the cake, she decided, as the cab made its way to the restaurant. He was bringing his new wife with him, and

Chloe had yet to meet her. She would have thought she'd been jealous when she received the announcement that they'd been married in Jamaica, but that ship had sailed so many years ago, she could find nothing but joy in her heart for her friend.

Perhaps someday she'd bring the man of her dreams to lunch to meet Tyler. Someday.

TYLER'S WIFE was as genuine and as sweet as Tyler himself. And, from the way she hung on his every word, and his arm, Chloe knew they were truly in love.

She found that as he talked about opening ten more stores throughout the midwest, her thoughts wandered home again to the streets of Aubrey Heights. Certainly that was triggered by the snow falling outside the restaurant window.

But she thought of the little coffee shop in town, and the Christmas tree that had been erected in the corner of the store. She thought about Melanie Peet's little gift store and Abby Foster's candle store. She remembered them all decorated for Christmas.

She soon realized Tyler was talking about holiday scents and decor in his stores. No wonder her mind had wandered for a moment.

"We're going to fly down to Brazil after the first of the year to look at a new bean farm. We thought we'd take in a tour of some rainforests, too," Tyler said, and his new bride glowed next to him.

"That sounds fantastic."

"You should go with us. It would give you a new perspective on what we do—how we source our beans and what goes into our decisions."

Chloe was fully alert now. "That would be quite a trip."

"Think about it," Tyler's wife said. "The world is such a big place. You don't want to miss seeing any of it."

And how depressing was that?

Chloe had never traveled the world. She hardly made it out of state. Her world was her clients and her little apartment. But that was what she'd wanted, right?

"I'll give it some thought. I've never traveled like that before."

Tyler looked at his wife and then back at her. "We'd love to have you join us."

CHAPTER 16

*E*xamining the stitches in his forehead, Jason realized he'd been unproductive in his day. After he'd arranged meetings with the clients who had called that morning, he hadn't gotten much done. And tomorrow he had his appointment to have the stitches taken out, so that was going to cost him even more time.

He'd wanted to hit the gym after work, but it looked like a few miles on his Peloton bike at home was going to have to do.

Chloe had come back from lunch and promptly locked herself away in her office. It seemed to be her method and perhaps why she was so good at her job. He'd seen Jody come and go from Chloe's office, always shutting the door behind her, giving him a big signal that she didn't want to be interrupted.

Jason took a conference call in the board room toward the end of the day, waving at Byron Mason as he walked by the bay of windows and toward the elevator. He watched as Byron tapped on Chloe's door, opened it just enough to talk to her, and then headed out of the office.

While he conducted business with one of his

former clients, Jason watched as the office began to empty, until once again only he and Chloe remained.

When he finalized the call, he realized that William still lurked in the office, when he opened the door and plopped down in one of the many empty chairs at the table.

"You've been a busy man today," William said, smiling as he picked up one of the pens from the cup on the table and twirled it between his fingers.

"I've had a lot of former clients call today looking for new representation, here."

"That's fantastic to hear. Gotta love a guy who has a lot going for him." William turned and leaned in on the table with his elbows. "How's *Pop!* coming along?"

"Chloe is working hard on it. She and Gloria seem to have a good relationship. She's finalizing the plans right now. After the first of the year we'll be ready to hit the ground running."

William nodded his head slowly. "Do you think she can handle the size of the account? I mean..." He didn't finish his thought, only shrugged.

Jason wasn't quite sure what kind of answer William was searching for. "I think Chloe is going to handle this just fine. She knows her business and the team we build for this account will be top of the line. *Pop! Cosmetics* is going to bring in a lot of revenue for the firm."

A smile formed on William's lips as he pushed himself back from the table. "You sound like you have a thumb on everything going on."

"That's why you hired me."

"Sure is. See ya tomorrow."

Jason watched as William walked out of the office past Chloe's door, and he didn't stop to say goodbye.

By seven o'clock, he was ready to call it a day. He could have left the office an hour earlier, but he was compelled to stay since Chloe's light was still on in her office.

Well, he didn't have to stay. She'd been putting in long hours for years before he got there. No need to babysit her, he thought, and he gathered his coat and started out just as her office door opened and she screamed as she saw him in the hallway.

"Damnit!" She pressed her hand to her chest. "I have got to remember that you stay later than anyone else in the history of this company."

"Everyone but you."

"I have a lot of work to do. Besides, maybe you should tell me when you're here past six or going to be in on Sundays. One of these days I might kill you with something rather than simply marring your face," she offered, looking up at his stitches.

"They come out tomorrow."

"Good. The guilt is horrible every time I see them."

Jason glanced in her office and noticed the mountain of paper on her desk. "What are you working on?"

"I just finished up the plan for *Pop! Cosmetics*. I was going over some of the schedules for *Needed Bean Coffee* and *Grandma Gert's Cookies*. I was trying to find a connection where we could get the two of them to do some cross promotions in their stores."

"Fabulous idea."

"Have you ever been to Brazil?"

The question caught him off guard and he chuckled. "No. I've been to Mexico on vacation once," but he wasn't going to delve into that disaster. "Otherwise, my mother's house in Florida is the furthest south I've ever been. Why do you ask?"

"Tyler invited me to Brazil after the first of the year. He's looking at a new bean farm. I was reminded that the world is a big place and I shouldn't miss seeing any of it."

There was a heat that formed in Jason's chest. He had to assume it was the hot dog he'd eaten for lunch and not some crazy jealousy that had arisen because Chloe's ex-boyfriend from college had invited her to travel to Brazil with him.

Oh, who was he kidding? That was exactly what had spurred it. The last thing he wanted to think about was Chloe going to Brazil with another man.

"Why don't you close up and let me take you to dinner," he proposed, realizing it was a date he was asking for.

"I have a cup of ramen in the break room calling my name. I'm good. But thanks for the offer."

It would be stupid for him to decide to take off his coat now and go back to his office—it would appear desperate, but then, so was asking her to dinner in the manner in which he had.

"Are you sure? None of this can wait until tomorrow?"

"I don't like to leave my office looking like it does right now," she admitted as her cell phone rang and it played a Christmas song. "*Walking in a Winter Wonderland.* It's my mother. It's her favorite song."

"Oh, you'd better get that then. I'll see you in the morning."

Chloe nodded and went back into her office to answer the phone.

Jason walked slowly to the elevators wondering how he could possibly steal just a few more minutes with her.

"I had a great lunch. Tyler is headed to Brazil after the first of the year and he invited me to go," she said and then paused. "He's doing great, Mom. And he said we would have a great time."

The elevator opened and Jason stepped in. That heat intensified in his chest. He was going to need to take a few days away to avoid stepping across that line with Chloe. He'd promised himself not to ever get involved with someone from work again—then he'd decided that was bullshit—but she was occupying too much of his mind. How was he not going to let her know how he felt?

CHAPTER 17

From the moment Chloe walked into the office, she'd been bombarded with phone calls requesting meetings, messages from current clients, and Gloria had called her on her cell phone three times to run some ideas by her.

This was the life she'd worked so hard for. Having the title of Account Manager suddenly didn't seem so important, especially since the current person managing all the accounts was willing to help her out.

She had to admit to herself that she enjoyed his company and his willingness to make sure *Pop! Cosmetics* was well taken care of. He understood what it could bring to the firm. Sure, there was probably some satisfaction in knowing that *Deb* hadn't gotten her hands on it.

Chloe looked at her watch and realized it was ten past ten. She'd gotten to the office at seven, and still hadn't seen Jason walk by her window, as he did every morning as if he were checking in. She noticed, though she never looked up to acknowledge him when he did so.

They'd had a few meals, and shared some personal stories, and a cab ride home. They had their minor victory, and of course that very intimate cele-bratory hug in his office.

That had been on her mind more than it should have. She couldn't help but think of his expression when she'd told him about her lunch with Tyler Ashby too. Certainly she'd mentioned that Tyler's wife had gone with them. Hadn't she?

Perhaps she'd fetch her next cup of coffee this morning, before Jody decided it was time for her to have some hydration.

Chloe walked the long way around the office, purposely meaning to go by Jason's office. The lights were all off, and the door was shut.

He was probably still at the doctor's office having his stitches removed. Hopefully, he wouldn't have a large scar, like her father did when he got stitches on his forehead. Though, when she thought about it, it did give her father a unique and rugged look. Perhaps it would make Jason even sexier. The thought filled her cheeks with heat, and she wondered where that had crept in from. Oh, she thought he was attractive, but sexy? She needed to get out of the office more often.

Chuckling to herself, she passed by Byron Ma-son's office just as the door opened.

"Oh, Chloe, I'm so glad I ran into you," Byron said as he stepped out into the hallway. "Getting yourself a cup of coffee?"

"I was just headed that way. Can I get you one as well?" She offered.

"That would be fantastic," Byron said as he placed his hand on her shoulder. "If you don't mind, would you bring back two cups? Oh, and a pocket full of sugar packets."

The smile that came to Chloe's lips was instanta-neous. "I can do that for you. I'll be right back."

Byron slipped back into his office and shut the door. Chloe walked to the break room wondering who he was trying to impress behind closed doors. She was happy to know he was still working accounts, and not just handing everything over to his son. Though William Mason knew the business, he wasn't as smooth or as kind as his father.

Chloe had learned to deal with William Mason, but she did enjoy the years before he had joined the firm. Everything had to change, she knew. Family businesses, no matter what they were, meant that more family would join in and they would take the positions other people were vying for.

Chloe filled her coffee mug, the one her mother had sent her from Aubrey Heights with the bridge that crossed from one side to the other etched with gold paint. She placed it on a small tray that they kept on top of the refrigerator and filled two more cups of coffee. She took a handful of sugar packets, and a few of the small creamers, and placed them on the tray as well. As she walked out, she turned back and picked up a few stir sticks adding them to the pile on the tray. She noticed there were a few donuts left in the box that Jody had brought that morning. Suddenly, her stomach growled. Had she eaten breakfast? No, she'd forgotten. Maybe she would eat one on her walk down the hall.

Chloe looked in the box and pulled out a small powdered donut. She took one small bite, and then set it on a napkin and added it to the tray with coffee.

She walked back down the hall toward Byron's office. Taking one more small bite of her donut, she tapped on the door.

When the door opened, it was William standing on the other side. Inside the office, Byron sat behind his desk, and a woman sat in the chair facing him.

When she turned around, Chloe choked on the powder from the donut.

Turning her head to cough, she held out the tray for William to take. Once her hands were free, she reached for her cup of coffee and took a sip to wash down the powder.

"Are you doing okay?" Byron asked from inside his office.

"I'm fine. Too much powder. Enjoy your coffee," she said and turned to walk back to her office.

"Chloe," William called. "We'd like you to join us."

Chloe could feel the heat rise in her cheeks again, only this time it wasn't because she was having romantic thoughts about Jason. It was because she had seen who was sitting in that chair in Byron's office. No, she didn't want to join them. But, she turned around, smiled at William, and walked into the office where Deborah King sat smiling smugly at her.

Byron handed Deborah one of the cups of coffee Chloe had poured.

"Thank you, darling," Deborah said smoothly and then adjusted her look back toward Chloe.

"Chloe," Byron Mason began, "I want you to meet Deborah King."

Deborah held out her hand and Chloe attempted to control hers noting that it shook. "Oh, Chloe and I have met. It seems we're both friends with Gloria Vandenberg."

William closed office door, blocking Chloe's only exit. "That's right, you both have worked with Gloria." He walked to the open chair and plopped down in it. "You'll work well together," he offered crossing one leg over the other and sitting back in his chair.

Chloe was sure the look on his face was one of amusement. Certainly, both of these men had to know that Deborah was the other runner for the account. And, they had to know that she wasn't chosen by Gloria, Chloe was.

Chloe took a sip of her coffee and looked in Byron's direction. "We'll work well together?"

Byron smiled up at her, genuinely excited about whatever he was about to tell her. "We've just acquired Ms. King at the firm. She comes highly recommended. I think she'll be a great asset."

Certainly they had to be kidding, weren't they? Deborah King, *Deb*, was not part of their team. She was the enemy. She was the cause of Jason leaving the last firm he worked for. She was a sexual predator. Didn't they know anything about this woman?

Chloe caught the look on William's face. Yes, he knew all about this woman. It was William's father who had been swindled to hire her. Seriously, they expected her to work with her?

"Shouldn't our Account Manager be in on this?" she asked, hoping that Jason would walk through the door at that moment.

William adjusted the large Rolex on his wrist, and then focused on her, those blue eyes piercing right through her.

"He had an appointment this morning, and then took a couple personal days to make a long weekend. He'll be informed."

A couple of personal days to make a long weekend, she replayed it over in her head. Chloe was facing this alone, and Jason probably had no idea. Or did he? Was this all part of his plan too? Was everything he told her about Deborah a lie? Have they been planning on taking over *Mason Arts* this entire time?

Chloe felt like an idiot.

"Welcome to the firm, Ms. King," she said trying to control her voice, and her hands that were cupped around her mug. "I'm sure you'll be very happy here."

Deborah smiled with those red painted lips, and Chloe felt her chest tighten. "I'm sure I will be."

Chloe turned and walked out of the office. She knew what having Deborah King sitting in that office meant. All of the years of dedication and hard work weren't going to pay off this time either.

CHAPTER 18

*E*very time Jason passed the small decorative mirror in his hallway, he looked at the mark that was left from the stitches that had been taken out that morning. In a few weeks no one would know that he been the victim of a wayward stapler.

The very thought had him chuckling to himself as he carried his water bottle toward his stationary bike. William had been quick to offer him a few personal days after he was done the doctor's office. Considering the fact he'd been having those thoughts about Chloe, and he didn't know what to do with them, he was grateful to have the time off. Maybe, by Monday, he would be ready to face Chloe and her impending trip to Brazil with Tyler Ashby.

Tyler Ashby, the name seemed so presumptuous. When he thought about what Ashby had to offer Chloe, Jason felt small. He was really only a hardworking slob in the suit, with a bachelor's degree. Tyler Ashby ran an empire and took trips to Brazil. Really, what was more appealing?

Jason climbed on his bike and tapped the attached screen to start his workout. A good hour on the bike while he looked out over the city and the people trudging through the snow would steady his nerves. When he was done, he would take a shower and call his mother. She sent him a very detailed email about how she wanted him to join her for Christmas. Depending on where all of the accounts were when he got back the following week, he'd make some plans. But, since his job was new, it had to be business first.

And he hoped by Monday, he'd be over his infatuation with Chloe and when she told him she was heading to Brazil, it wouldn't matter.

* * *

CHLOE KEPT to herself in her office, the door shut and locked. She didn't even want to see Jody's happy face walk through the door.

Her desk was piled with papers, as she still tried to decide how she could get *Needed Bean Coffee* and *Grandma Gert's Cookies* to work together to maximize their marketing budget. But, her head wasn't in the game.

Her mind was on Deborah King sitting in Byron Mason's office, and on the fact that Deborah King was there to take over her job. Wasn't it enough that they had hired Jason and not given her the position? At what point was it all too much? Where was the loyalty? She'd been loyal. She'd worked her ass off.

Who was there before everyone else in the morning? She was. Who was there every night after everyone had gone home? That was also her.

She had missed Thanksgiving dinner with her family to be at work. Seriously, they needed to cut her some slack.

Chloe nearly screamed when there was a knock at the door, and someone trying to open it. Angrily, she stood from behind her desk and walked across the office. Unlocking the door, she swung it open and saw the very pleasant smile of Byron Mason on the other side.

"You're working so hard, you locked yourself in your office," he said smiling up at her. "You're a good girl. I'm glad to have you on our team."

The man was senile, she decided as she smiled back at him, even if the smile was forced. "Thank you. I appreciate that."

Byron Mason took her hand and gave it a pat. "The wife and I are headed out for the weekend. We're headed up to Vermont for some Christmas festivities."

The very thought of it made her miss home, and the streets of Aubrey Heights. She sure could do with some Christmas festivities and holiday spirit at that moment.

"Enjoy yourself. That sounds delightful."

"I'll see you on Monday," he promised as he walked toward the elevator, his coat draped over his arm.

Jody's head perked up from behind her cubicle wall. "I brought in a crockpot full of corn chowder for lunch. Interested?"

Chloe's stomach growled, and she nodded. "I think that would be delightful. Thank you."

Jody smiled and hurried off toward the break room.

Chloe stood in the doorway and took in the sights and sounds of the office around her. Everyone had their own agenda, and some of them were not in sync with hers. When they pooled their team together to execute Gloria's marketing plan, would they all sync then? What part would Deborah play in all of that? What part would Chloe play?

She watched Jody's bright hair bounce as she

walked back toward her with a bowl of soup in her hands. "Here's a bowl," she said as she handed it to Chloe. "And I filled my pockets with crackers just in case you wanted some."

Chloe chuckled, and held out her hand. "Thank you for always taking care of me, Jody."

"You're a hard worker. You deserve to have someone look after you. Let me know if you need anything else, or even if you want a refill. There's plenty back there."

"Thank you," she said sincerely as she turned back toward her desk to eat her soup in silence.

THE DAY SLIPPED AWAY, just as they all did eventually. Jody had poked her head into Chloe's office and waved goodbye after checking in to make sure she didn't need any more soup, or another cup of coffee. Then, the office grew silent and Chloe got back to work.

Jody had left the office door open, which was un-characteristic. Chloe often thought of her as the gate-keeper. Jody would keep unwanted guests out of Chloe's office, and she never asked her to do so, but she appreciated it.

There were still people talking, and Chloe knew she wasn't completely alone. She also knew that Jason was not one of the people staying after work to finish.

She hated to admit that she had missed him all day. She had only known him a week, and already she had caused him bodily harm, learned some of his deepest secrets, and eaten many meals with him. Chloe felt as if they had known each other for years. Of course, had they known each other for years, he wouldn't have looked at herself strangely when she mentioned Tyler's invitation to Brazil. Had that been resentment because it would take her away from work? Could it have been jealousy?

Certainly it wasn't jealousy. What would he have to be jealous over? Except for her trip to Brazil that is. Then she thought of Deborah sitting in Byron's office. He had to know she was coming. Why else would he have taken time off? He knew how Chloe felt about her, and yet now they were teammates?

The thought churned her stomach. She worked too damn hard to have Deborah King walk in and be part of what she'd built. Chloe had worked with Gloria to get that account, no one else. She would be damned if she wasn't in charge of it. She had half a mind to look up Jason's address, head over to his house, and give him a piece of her mind. In fact, she thought that was exactly what she would do. He owed her an explanation.

Chloe stood from behind her desk with all intent on going through the files in the H.R. office. However, she stopped her progression when William walked by her door.

"I'm glad you're still here. I wanted to talk to you."

He closed the door behind him, and Chloe fisted her hands to her side.

"Can you talk to me tomorrow? I still have a lot of work I need to finish up on."

Byron crossed his arms over his chest and shook his head. "I think you're going to find your agenda will be very free."

"I beg your pardon?"

"Listen, babe," he lifted his hands as if he were a preacher. "The firm is taking a different direction. We need to be a little more cutthroat, a little more aggressive."

She pushed past the part where he called her babe

and gritted her teeth. "Fine, I'll make sure to be a little more cutthroat and aggressive."

William wagged his finger at her. "I don't think you understand. You're old school. And though there is a time and place for that, we are not looking at managing the accounts of coffee shops and cookie grandmas. We are stepping up our game. *Pop! Cosmetics* is putting us on the map, at the forefront."

"And I sealed the deal. I got that account. I worked my ass off for that account."

William examined his fingers, as if he just got a new manicure. "Yeah, you did good. But, I think it's time we part ways. Don't you?"

Her fingernails dug into her palms as she tightened her fists. "Part ways? What exactly does that mean?"

"And I thought you were the one with the Masters degree. It means your services are no longer required at *Mason Arts*. You have tonight to pack up your desk. All of your accounts are taken care of, even your coffee and cookie accounts."

Chloe took in a deep, ragged breath and placed her palms flat on the top of her desk. "You're firing me?"

"I thought parting ways was a nicer way to say that, but if you like it to be blunt, then yeah, you're fired."

"Why?"

"Your productivity is down, you spent too much time going after *Pop!* That deal should've been locked up a month ago and we should've already been moving on it."

"There were other people involved in it. Gloria Vandenberg was choosing between our firm and another firm. She chose us."

"She did choose *us*," he said sternly. "And we'll take

it from here. No hard feelings, doll. I happen to know there's a few openings at *Stockton Advertising*." He tapped his hand on the door jamb as if to say he was done with their conversation and walked to the elevator and disappeared.

CHAPTER 19

*C*hloe lowered herself down to the chair behind her desk. Her entire body shook, and tears clogged her throat, though they didn't reach her eyes. Anger, the vile taste of anger filled her mouth where words should be. Oh no, she was not going down without a fight. She had worked her ass off for that firm, and he was going to dismiss her just like that?

No, no, no.

Her first call was to Gloria Vandenberg, but she wasn't in the office and she didn't answer her personal cell phone. She called Tyler and let him know they had let her go from the firm, and he promised he'd pull his advertising dollars the first thing Monday morning. He wasn't gonna work with the company that discarded their employees like the Masons did.

The next few phone calls weren't quite the same. Though they appreciated the information, they were staying with the firm through their contract, and then maybe they shop around.

The outer office was now dark, as maintenance

had turned off the lights. Chloe sat alone in the office, which had been her home for nearly the past decade. What was done was done, she decided. She let out a deflated breath.

What was the use in sitting there and being angry? The Masons didn't want her. Jason didn't want to work with her. Deborah was there to take over. No one needed her anymore. Who would've thought that she'd be washed up just shy of thirty?

Chloe turned in her chair to pick up an empty paper box she had meant to discard but now she would pack in. Looking out the window, for what she knew would be one of the last times, she watched as the snow fell, illuminated by the streetlights.

Unemployed at Christmas time, she thought to herself. Unless she wanted to work part-time retail, she had nothing. No one hired someone a few weeks before Christmas. Maybe she would take this as an opportunity and just go home. The people of Aubrey Heights would fill that void in her. The sense of community, the feeling of Christmas, it would all surround her. The big city and its cold and callous people could just be put on hold until after the new year, she decided, as she put her personal items in the box.

Maybe she was meant for something better than selling cosmetics to the masses. Maybe deep down inside her she was still just a small town girl who wanted to celebrate Christmas all year round.

Chloe picked up the stapler from her desk, intent on putting it in the box, she stopped. She supposed that was corporate property, and she set it back down but not until she had run her fingers over it and thought about the day she had hit Jason with it.

She hated to think he was in on the takeover of

Mason Arts. Again, she had truly missed him not being there. Obviously, it wasn't meant for them to work together. Things were different now, especially since William was running the show and Deborah was now involved.

Chloe's phone rang, and she pulled it from her purse. She smiled as she looked down at the caller ID and saw Tyler's face pop up on the screen.

"Is your passport current?" he asked before she could even say hello.

She had no stamps in her passport, though she did keep it up-to-date. "It's current."

"We are taking off January fifteenth. I happen to know that your schedule is totally free, as per our conversation earlier," he joked. "You're going with us to Brazil, and I'm not going to take no for an answer."

"Tyler, as much as I love that, I'm sure your wife would prefer you not take me along, and I'm prob-ably going to need to have a new job by then and not going to be able to take off work."

"You have a job. I want you internally."

Chloe leaned back in her chair and took in the sight of her half-dismantled office. "What do you mean?"

"You can work from anywhere in the world, if you want. *Needed Bean Coffee* could use an internal Adver-tising Director. I've already talked to my dad about it. I'll give you until after Christmas to decide, but I think you should think about it."

Chloe laughed, and laughed hard. Who would have thought an ex-boyfriend from college would be her saving grace. "You're serious? You're offering me a job?"

"Ah, a new career." Tyler left on the other end of the phone. "You think about it. I'd love to have you."

"I'll think about it," she said feeling the smile tug at her lips. "This means a lot to me."

"Are you headed back home?" he asked as if she'd already mentioned it, but she hadn't. He simply knew her that well.

"It's Christmas and Aubrey Heights, where else in the world what I want to be?"

"I have been telling Gwendolyn all about it," he said as he sighed into the phone. "I think maybe we will come and visit you, right before Christmas."

"I can't think of anything better." Chloe took a deep breath and let all the uncertainty settle around her. "Tyler, thank you."

"I'll talk to you soon," he said before the line went dead.

Chloe tucked her phone back into her purse and finished loading the box with her personal items. She had the contacts she needed in her phone, and everything else belonged to the company.

Instead of locking her office door, she set the key on her desk. She stopped by Jody's desk, and took a sticky note and wrote *thank you* on it and signed it. She left it for Jody to find the next day, and then she turned toward the elevator.

She pushed the arrow that would summon the elevator to take her down to the lobby. As she waited, she looked around the dark office and she felt the sadness tug at her. Change was good, she reminded herself. She would embrace the change that had come her way without her asking for it.

Tomorrow she would make the drive back home, and plan to stay until the new year. It sounded like maybe she already had a new job, and maybe she could talk Tyler into letting her work from Aubrey Heights and not in the city. Could she do that? Could she handle small town again?

The elevator door opened and Chloe stepped in. As the door closed, she resigned to the fact that it was worth a try. The big city had squashed her spirit. Perhaps she needed her small town to build it again.

CHAPTER 20

*F*our days off in a row was unheard of in Jason's professional life. It was no wonder his mother was always after him to take it easy. He had hardly known what to do with himself after he took a couple personal days and then laid low for the weekend.

It had taken everything inside of him to not go into the office on Sunday, as it had become quite a ritual. Instead, he went Christmas shopping. Now, with a small tree on his coffee table, and a few ill-wrapped gifts underneath, he felt as though the Christmas spirit had touched him.

Usually, he was on Amazon frantically shopping for Christmas and having it shipped. He did splurge for gift wrap, but this year he had done it himself. Now all he needed to do was to remember to ship it.

Maybe he could play the woeful man in this scenario. He'd stayed away from the office, and Chloe, for four days. He'd gotten over the tug she had on him, emotionally. He felt as though he could go into the office as her coworker. However, wouldn't it be nice to have lunch together, and maybe she could help him ship those packages?

He rinsed out his coffee cup and put it in the dishwasher. Grabbing a banana off the counter, he pulled on his coat, hung his scarf around his neck, and headed out into the cold.

The snow had kicked up, and a freeze had taken hold. It was days like this he liked city-living less than usual. Sure, in a suburb, he'd have had to brush off his car to make the drive into work. But, he could enjoy his cup of coffee, listen to his music, and stay warm until he hit the parking lot of his office. As it was, he had twenty-three blocks to walk in misery.

As he passed people on the street, bundled from head to toe, he realized he was warm from the inside out. There were no stitches left in his forehead, there was warm coffee waiting at the office, and knowing that Chloe was going to ignore his wave as he passed by her door had him nearly laughing out loud.

He looked forward to getting to work on the *Pop! Cosmetics* account fully after the first of the year. Seeing Chloe in full action, in charge of the team, excited him. The entire process excited him. He'd seen her work ethic, and how she buried herself in her office for hours on end. She had what it took to run the campaign, and to manage the people. This was going to be her shining moment, and he was happy to be part of it.

Did the people of Aubrey Heights know what a gem Chloe was? Had she worked in one of those small stores growing up, and had they taught her leadership?

Had she taken Tyler Ashby back to Aubrey Heights in college?

What the hell did that matter? Jason walked around a man digging through a trashcan in the doorway of the building.

He thought in four days he had managed to wrap

his head around the fact that Chloe Richardson was only a coworker. If that were the case, it wouldn't matter if she had taken Tyler Ashby back to Aubrey Heights in college. It wouldn't matter if she took Tyler Ashby home with her last night.

But for some reason it did matter.

The warmth that he had felt during his walk, disappeared as he walked through the front door into the elevator. He didn't want Chloe to just be a coworker. But he had made himself a promise not to get involved with anyone from work, ever again.

This was going to take even more thought.

THE OFFICE WAS ALREADY BUSTLING when the doors to the elevator opened. As he stepped off the elevator, Jody quickly caught his eye. Usually, she welcomed him with a smile, a muffin and if she had one, and sometimes even a story about her grandson. Today the woman looked absolutely frazzled. She couldn't have even been at work more than fifteen minutes, but her day didn't seem to be going quite right.

One sight Jason was not accustomed to, was seeing Chloe's office door open. Usually, she would've been there for hours already, and her door would be closed because she would be busy working on details.

However, he could see the door was open, the blinds were up, and there was someone sitting in her chair. He walked closer to the door and stood there. When the woman seated behind the desk lifted her head, Jason thought perhaps his heart had stopped.

"I would've expected to see you hours ago," Deborah King said as she stood from behind the desk. "You usually worked on Sundays and were always at work bright and early on Monday mornings. What changed, Jason? You're not getting sloppy, are you?"

He stepped into the office and shut the door behind him. "What are you doing here?"

The devilish smile that the woman wielded formed on her red painted lips. "Perhaps you should check your emails on the weekend. Were you busy with extracurricular activities?"

"What I do on the weekend doesn't affect you. What are you doing here? And what are you doing in Chloe's office?"

Deborah sat back down in the chair and folded her arms on top of the desk. Tapping her bright red fingernails on the wood, she looked up at him. "Check the name on the door of the office, darling. I thought you more observant than that."

Jason's heart began to pound in his chest as he opened the office door and looked at the nameplate.

DEBORAH KING

"That's right. Maybe you should get to your office and get busy before they change the name on your door too," she said snidely.

Jason gripped his messenger bag tightly in his hand. He didn't like where this was going, not one bit. He had moved to *Mason Arts* to get away from the woman staring at him as he walked away. It would be a cold day in hell when he worked with her again.

Jason's step quickened as he walked toward his office. His name was still on the door, and it was still closed. As he took his keys from his pocket, and unlocked the door, Byron Mason stepped out of his office.

"Good morning, Jason. How is your extended weekend? Tell me you did something fun," the old man smiled optimistically.

"I just relaxed. Nothing fun."

"That's too bad."

Jason watched the man watching him. He needed some answers. "Have you spoken to Chloe this morning?"

Now the older man's face retracted its smile. "I'm sorry you didn't know, but Chloe resigned."

"Resigned? She just landed the biggest deal this firm has ever had. Why would she resign?"

The man standing in front of him shrugged. "Chloe has been with us that she was in college. She was an intern. A spark of brilliance, that's what she is. We brought in a new colleague, and William told me Chloe didn't like it, and resigned."

Jason bit down on his lip and pushed open his office to work. He doubted very highly that Chloe simply walked away from a job she loved as much as she did.

"I assume Deborah King is taking Chloe's place?"

The smile was back on Byron Mason's face. "Do you know Deb? Oh wait, you've worked together before, right?"

"Right," Jason got out the word. "I passed by her this morning, in Chloe's office."

Byron nodded. "We decided it was the best place for her to be. I'm sorry Chloe felt as though she had to go. I'll miss her. I've never seen anyone work as hard as that girl."

Byron retreated back into his office and closed the door. Jason did the same.

He looked out over the white blanket covering the city and wondered where Chloe Richardson had gone.

a fresh new blanket of snow covered the ground. Chloe held her coffee mug in her hand and looked out the kitchen window. The backyard where she used to run as a child was now a white wonderland begging for her to come back. Would it be so bad to jump into the snow and create a snowman like she would have years ago? Maybe a snow angel, or an igloo. Perhaps that was exactly what she needed. A few minutes of being childish and foolish would make her feel much better, she decided. She took another sip of her very grownup coffee and then considered that hot chocolate would have been equally appropriate, and tastier.

The adult Chloe wasn't having any fun at the moment. She still couldn't believe that William had fired her in the way that he had. He didn't document anything, or send her to H.R. He'd just dismissed her.

Maybe what she couldn't believe was that she hadn't fought him. She should have called his father, raised a ruckus, and stood her ground. She should have been in that office that morning talking to H.R. herself. But she hadn't. Instead she'd packed up nearly a decade of work and dumped it into a box, which now cluttered her kitchen counter back in the city.

Chloe poured the rest of the coffee down the sink and rinsed her mug. Now she stood in her parents' home having a pity party.

After William Mason had left the office, she had packed up her belongings, gone home, and packed a suitcase. She was in her car four o'clock the next morning and headed back to Aubrey Heights. One thing was for sure, she'd always belong in Aubrey Heights.

Now, as she wandered through the quiet house, she wondered what Jason thought when he got to work that morning. Or, had he been in on it the entire time?

Chloe plopped down on her mother's sofa and picked up a People magazine that laid on the end table. Flipping through the pages she looked at the models, their makeup, and the parties. Had she stayed at *Mason Arts*, would Gloria Vandenberg have invited her to some of these parties? Would she have walked red carpets? Would she have had her picture taken by the paparazzi, simply because of the company she was keeping?

She tossed the magazine back on the table. Now she was just digging for things to feel pitiful over.

What she had to remember was that she had a job offer. Not only did she have a job offer, she had an invitation to go to Brazil, of all places. *Needed Bean Coffee* was doing some good in the world. She was asked to be part of that.

A warmth she hadn't felt in days crept back through her. Who cared if Jason Mitchell was part of her getting fired? Who cared that Deborah King was probably sitting at her desk? Who cared that William Mason thought so little of her that he dismissed her?

Tyler Ashby and his beautiful wife Gwendolyn wanted her to be part of what they had.

With a new sense of urgency in her life, Chloe walked to the back door, and threw on her coat. She would ride out the holidays in Aubrey Heights, and then she would call Tyler and take him up on his offer. For now, she was going to go into town and spend a few dollars on a fancy coffee—or hot chocolate—before heading over to Melanie Peet's quaint little gift shop to ask for a job to get her through the holidays.

* * *

JASON HAD MEANT to dig up Chloe's phone number again, but he got caught up in contracts with a new client. At lunch, he'd planned to take a cab to her apartment. He could remember the building, and from there, he'd figure it out, but *Deb* had called an internal meeting and William made sure Jason was present.

As the sky outside his window grew darker, and he'd seen Jody rise from her desk with her coat on, he knew the office would quickly empty out. He planned to be on those elevators with the masses for the first time since he'd set foot into the offices of *Mason Arts*. No late nights for him as long as *Deb* was around.

Making his way around the desk, he picked up his messenger bag, and pulled his coat from the hook by the door just as it opened. Unwelcome and unwanted, Deborah King walked in and shut the door behind her.

"We need to go over this contract proposal for *Giant Auto*," she said as she dropped a file on his desk and then fell into one of the empty chairs in Jason's office.

"Tomorrow. Time to go home now."

"Time to work, Jason, or did you forget how to do that? You never leave at the first bell," she taunted. "Let's go over this."

At that moment he was tempted to simply walk out. She wasn't his boss. She wasn't his manager. As far as he was concerned, he still held rank, but *Giant Auto* had followed him to *Mason Arts*, and he owed it to them to give them the service they expected from him.

"You have twenty minutes."

Deborah crossed one leg over the other and bounced her foot. "Do you have a date?"

"It's none of your business what I have. Work is work, and my life is just that. My life."

"It never was before, Jason. Don't you remember our long nights in the office?"

He could feel the heat rising in his face as he swallowed down the ball of anger that choked him.

Walking back to the door of his office, he hung his coat back on the rack, and opened the door before taking his seat behind his desk.

There were not going to be any blurred lines this time. He was in control here. And he would write the rules of the relationship they would have—which would be strictly a working relationship.

CHAPTER 22

$\mathcal{A}$n hour later, Deborah sauntered out of his office and Jason leaned back in his chair, exhausted. The woman could nitpick every detail of any document associated with an account. He'd given her twenty minutes and she'd taken an entire hour out of his evening, and he was fuming over it.

Jason walked to the door and pulled his coat off the rack again. He swung it on and wrapped his scarf around his neck before fetching his messenger bag and heading toward the elevator.

He'd walked the other direction on purpose, so as to not walk by Chloe's... Deborah's office. There was no way in hell he was going to talk to her for one more moment.

Pushing the button on the elevator, he impatiently waited for it to arrive. When it did, he hurried in and pushed the button.

Just as the doors were closing, a hand slid between the doors to open them and Deborah stepped inside.

"Might as well ride together, right?" she said as she tossed her hair over her shoulder and stood right next to Jason in the otherwise empty elevator. "Like old times, eh?"

Jason clenched his jaw. No, he wasn't going to engage the woman in conversation, especially when he knew where she was going with it.

Realizing she was nearly touching him by her proximity, he managed to inch away slightly, only to have her close the gap between them.

He watched the numbers on the elevator count down. They were almost to the lobby when he noticed her reach for the toggle switch that stopped the elevator between floors, and the car came to a halt.

Gripping his messenger bag in his hand, he turned his furious attention to her and only grew angrier when she smiled.

"Your empty claims of what happened between us before don't scare me, Jason. You were equal parts to blame for the failure of my marriage."

"I wasn't aware you were still married when that started."

"But you learned and were still involved."

Jason moved to start the elevator's descent again, but Deborah blocked his advance with her body.

"I'm done, Deborah. Release the elevator."

She laughed as if she were a villain in an animated movie. "Don't tell me you're not interested in me anymore. I wouldn't believe you if you did."

"My interests are directed elsewhere."

She tapped her red nail against the toggle, not yet releasing it. "Where are they directed?"

"None of your business."

"Chloe Richardson?"

Hearing Chloe's name on the lips of the vixen before him made him ill.

"As I said, none of your business."

Deborah clicked the toggle back and the elevator

jolted back to life. "Oh, darling, it is my business. After all, she left her job wide open for me. Honestly, how can you be interested in someone who is not very serious about her career? One day with me in the office, and she quit."

"I think there's more to it than that."

"She's threatened. I'm healthy competition. I guess she couldn't handle it."

The numbers counted down and the display finally showed L. The moment the doors opened, Jason slid through them and kept walking.

"I'll see you tomorrow," she called after him, but he continued to walk out of the building.

It was dark outside, and snow had started again. Jason waved at the nearest taxi, and it pulled over for him. He gave the driver directions to the nearest intersection he could remember to Chloe's building. Less than ten minutes later, he paid his tab, and climbed out into the snow.

Standing in the dark, with only streetlights to illuminate the addresses, he counted buildings until he thought he knew which one was hers. An old brownstone with multiple units. He walked up the steps and looked at the names next to the buzzer. At least this part of his day had gone correctly. 2B—Richardson it said.

Sucking in a deep breath of cold air, Jason pressed the button. It buzzed, but there was no answer. He buzzed again, and still no answer.

Walking back to the street, he looked up at the windows. One set of windows was illuminated. The other set was dark.

At that moment someone walked out the door, and he hurried past them and up the stairs placing his phone to his ear. "Yeah, I'm coming in right now," he said to mislead Chloe's neighbor, he assumed, and make his way into the building.

He walked up the flight of steps and stopped at the door that said 2B. Scrubbing his hand over his face, he knocked. Again, there was no answer. Maybe, he would leave her his business card, then she would know he'd been there.

Jason dug his wallet out of his pocket and pulled out a business card just as the door across the hallway opened.

"You looking for Chloe?" An older lady stood in the doorway in a bathrobe.

"I am."

"Who are you?" she inquired quizzically.

Jason turned to the woman and gave her a warm smile. "My name is Jason Mitchell. I work with Chloe at the advertising agency."

The woman nodded slowly taking in the sight of him, as if she were committing it to memory. "Chloe isn't here."

Jason tucked his wallet back in his pocket. "She wasn't at work today. I thought I would come by and check on her."

"She left Friday. You should go home now."

Controlling his expression, as well as he could, he continued to smile. "She left on Friday?"

"Bright and early. Long before the sun. I'm taking care to gather her mail and water plants. I have a key. I'm not going to let you in, but I have a key."

"I don't want in. I just want to know that she's okay."

The woman opened her door just a bit more, and Jason took that as a good sign. "She went back home."

He thought for a moment about their conversation when they discussed where she was from. "Aubrey Heights."

The woman smiled now. "That's it. I expect she'll be gone through the holidays."

So she'd left her job, and gone back home. Why would she do that, he wondered?

Jason took the business card he had pulled from his wallet and handed it to the woman. "If you hear from Chloe, will you tell her I stopped by? I'm worried about her, and I just want to follow up."

The woman took the card and studied it, just as she had him. "Are you dating her?"

Jason chuckled. "No."

"Well, you should consider it. She doesn't have people check up on her. She could use someone like you."

He wanted to laugh, because he wasn't sure she needed anybody like him. But somehow, he had won the lady over. "Maybe you'll give me a good recommendation if you talk to her."

"Merry Christmas," the woman said before she shut her door.

"Merry Christmas," Jason repeated, only now remembering Christmas was just two weeks away.

He looked at his watch. It was nearly eight-thirty. There were some serious decisions to make before he went back into the office the next morning.

At that moment, he wished he had gotten her number. He'd made so many phone calls since he'd last called her, her number was buried in his phone anonymously. He supposed he could narrow it down, but...

He wished he had acted on those feelings he was having. Would it really have made a difference? Still, he couldn't believe Chloe had walked away from a job that she had invested so much time in. He didn't know her well, but he felt as if he did. He would guarantee there was more to the story.

As he walked down the street, toward the intersection, the snow picked up, but he didn't feel the cold or the wind. All he felt was the heartache of missing Chloe.

Perhaps it was stupid, but he was old enough to realize that you didn't let something good slip through your fingers. He'd been enamored with Chloe from the moment he met her. He reached his gloved hand to the scar now forming on his forehead. There would never be a day in his life when he wouldn't think of her.

Should he make the bold move and head to Aubrey Heights? Or should he go back into the office, deal with the situation at hand, and reconsider his lot in life?

He hailed the next taxi to come along and headed toward home. It was going to be a long night.

CHAPTER 23

*M*elanie Peet hadn't even the let Chloe finish her sentence when she had asked for a job, before throwing her arms around Chloe's neck and shouting, "Yes! Yes! Yes!"

Now, on her second day of work, Chloe dusted the display case closest to the front door. Looking outside onto the streets of Aubrey Heights, she smiled, taking pleasure in the sight of the winter wonderland.

New snow had fallen overnight, and even though the plow had cleared the road, the snow still glistened in the sunlight. Perhaps on any other weekday the people would've stayed home. But, with only two weeks until Christmas, tourists had flooded the small town to take in the holiday spirit.

Even on a Tuesday morning, she could hear carolers across the street. A chestnut vendor had opened up next to the coffee shop. The small ice-skating rink at the end of town was filled with students who were out of school. How had she ever left this? Oh, the city held its own charm, but nothing would ever be as magical as Christmas in Aubrey Heights. Or so she thought until the door opened and a man walked into the store.

"Jason?"

He pulled the stocking hat from his head and wiped his boots on the mat. "For a small town, you're hard to find."

She couldn't believe she was standing there looking at him. It was Tuesday. Tuesday near his lunchtime. Tuesday, when she knew there had been a meeting scheduled with Gloria Vandenberg at noon.

"What are you doing here?"

He smiled, and she wondered if he could see the bead of sweat she felt on her brow. "I came looking for you."

"Why?"

Jason chuckled. "You sure do ask a lot of questions. Do you have anything in the store I can ship to my mother in two weeks? I have a few things for her, but she likes when I overindulge."

When he tipped his head as if he were making sure she was awake, she realized she hadn't answered him. She stood there dumbfounded that he was even at the store.

"You came six hours to buy your mother something for Christmas?"

"Had to rent a car, too. I don't own a car."

Still, she stared at him in disbelief. "There was a meeting today. At noon."

Jason turned his wrist to look at his watch. "Looks like I missed it."

Melanie removed herself from her perch behind the cash register and walked toward them. "Hello," she said, and Jason turned his attention toward her.

"Hello," he repeated the greeting.

"Can I help you find anything?"

"I found what I came looking for." Jason shifted

his look back at Chloe. "Any chance you have a coffee break?"

The corners of Melanie's mouth turned upward into a grand smile Chloe noticed.

Taking the duster from Chloe's hand, Melanie looked at Jason. "They have fantastic hot chocolate and apple fritters you cannot pass up at the coffee shop. I'm good here, take as much time as you like," she directed her comments to Chloe.

Chloe turned to her and stared. What was she doing? This was no time to send her employee away to talk to a man. They had work to do.

"I'm not done yet," she scowled through gritted teeth.

Melanie nodded at her. "You are for right now. Take a break."

The humor on Jason's face was undeniable. She wasn't sure she should be angry at both of them or just at Melanie. Fine, she find out what he came for, though she couldn't imagine why he had driven so far.

"Let me get my coat."

When Chloe returned from the back with her coat on and her hat in her hands, she noticed the smile on Jason's face. There was some kind of contentment in his eyes, and a gentleness to him she'd only seen when he'd hugged her that day in his office. Shouldn't he be in a state of panic? He was missing a meeting—an important meeting.

"I'll be back in thirty minutes," Chloe said to Melanie and for Jason's sake as well.

Melanie gave her a nod and went back to her place behind the counter.

Pulling on her cap, Chloe walked past Jason and out onto the cold streets where tourists looked in the windows and carried shopping bags from each store.

Leaving for coffee in the middle of the day was asinine—as much so as Jason not being in the city at his meeting.

THE COFFEE SHOP WAS BUSTLING. A small quartet sang carols in the corner of the store and the scent of chocolate hit Jason the moment they opened the door.

Chloe hadn't said a word to him on the short walk over, but she'd talk to him soon. What choice did she have? Would she really turn him away after he'd driven that far to see her?

He followed her to the counter where she ordered a hot chocolate. As she reached for her money, he stepped up and ordered one as well, just as Melanie had recommended, and a fritter.

"We're both on the same ticket," he said as he pulled a twenty from his wallet and handed it to the young lady at the register.

"Thank you," Chloe said without looking up at him.

"You're welcome." As their order was fulfilled, he looked around and spotted a small booth in the back corner that was unoccupied. "Why don't we sit back there?"

"Fine."

Chloe picked up her drink from the counter and headed to the table while Jason waited for his fritter. When he had his order, he walked toward the table where Chloe sat, her hat still on, and her coat buttoned to the lapel.

"This has to be the cutest coffee shop I've ever been in," he said as he set down his items, pulled off his coat, and hung it on the back of the chair before taking a seat.

"It's very quaint," she said sharply before taking her first sip of her hot chocolate. "Why are you here?"

Well, it was a conversation starter for sure, he thought as he sipped the rich hot chocolate, making sure to not leave whipped cream lingering on his lip.

"I heard that you quit, and I wanted…"

Her hands gripped the sides of her cup, and as she raised it to her lips, he could see them trembling. "I quit, huh?" She muttered the words behind the cup before taking a sip.

"That's what I was told."

Controlled, she lowered the cup to the table and clasped her hands in her lap. "I was *excused* from my job by William Mason."

"Excused?"

"And I quote, *your services are no longer required at Mason Arts.*"

Jason eased back in his seat. "Byron told me you resigned."

Color filled her cheeks. "No surprise there. William has been trying to get rid of me since he started. Why fight it? No one wants to work with me, then why should they have to?" A tear formed in her eye and she wiped it away quickly before resting her arms on the table and beginning to shred her napkin between her fingers. "Gloria Vandenberg will be fine with the firm. Others will forget I even existed."

"Deborah King took over your office."

He watched as she shredded her napkin into even smaller bits.

"I'm glad she has a place to work."

"You don't have to be like that. You don't have to be strong and positive."

Her head darted up and her eyes locked with his. "You're right. I could find a corner and sit there and cry. Or, as I did, I could pick up my life, come back home, work through Christmas, and start fresh next year."

"I think that sounds like a nice plan."

"Good. I have your blessing," she said as she pushed her cup to the center of the table. "I have to get back to the store."

Before she could make her exit, Jason reached across the table to cover her hand with his. "Have dinner with me tonight. I'm staying at the Inn and I was assured they do an amazing dinner."

Chloe's shoulders dropped. "They do."

"So will you join me?"

"Don't you need to get back to the city?"

Jason shook his head. "I'm in no hurry. Have dinner with me."

Chloe lifted her eyes to look at the people that came and went from the shop, and then those walking on the street. When she let her eyes settle back on him, he found that they were warm and inviting now. Was she realizing he was there to be her friend?

"I'll meet you at the Inn at seven," she offered.

"I look forward to it."

Pulling her hand away from his, she stood. "Thank you for the drink." Biting down on her lip she took one more moment to look at him. "Your scar doesn't look too bad."

Jason chuckled as he lifted his fingers to his brow. "I considered the fact that I'd think of you every day of my life."

Her eyes grew wide. "I'm so sorry."

"Don't be. It was a good thought."

She seemed to be rendered speechless then as she turned and walked out of the coffee shop.

CHAPTER 24

*C*hloe knew that the only reason Melanie didn't say anything to her when she walked back into the store was because there was a line at the register and six others window shopping.

Quickly, Chloe discarded her coat in the back and headed to the floor to help the shoppers. Only at Christmas time, in a small Christmas town, could one hide out better than in the big city.

It was nearly four o'clock when the crowds dwindled. The sound of Santa's bells rang out beyond the door as he paraded with his elves away from the center of town and back to the North Pole for the night. Soon, small ensembles would gather on each end of town to entertain those who took in the spirit of Christmas in the dark with twinkling lights and warm smells from the vendors.

As Chloe untied her apron, seeing that Melanie's other employee was coming to take the evening shift, she started toward the back when Melanie cut off her exit with a can of Coke in her hand as if to bribe her to stay a few more minutes.

"I didn't get to hear about your coffee break."

"Nothing to hear about, I guess," Chloe said as she took the Coke from Melanie and slid past her.

But, her escape was useless. Melanie followed, closing the door behind her.

"C'mon. You're the small town girl that got away to the big city and now you're back here. Not only that, *hello!*, handsome stranger comes looking for you, too. You have a story and I want to hear it."

Chloe dropped into the chair at the small table they used for breaks and opened the can of Coke. "There's not much to tell. He's the man they hired to take the position I thought I was getting promoted for. I land the biggest account in the history of the firm, and suddenly I'm no longer an asset to the company, and they hire the woman he used to work with. The woman he told me harassed him and caused him to leave his job. It's just a lot to take in."

Melanie sat in the seat across the table from her. "He didn't seem like some vicious, corporate, kiss-ass."

Sipping from the can, Chloe gave that some thought. "He's not. I genuinely think he's a nice guy."

"And he's in Aubrey Heights why?"

"I have no idea. As far as I'm concerned, I owe him nothing and vice-versa. The account is in good hands with him. And, hell, I got my licks in. Did you see the fresh mark above his eye? I did that."

"You did that? What, did you take a hockey stick to his face?"

Chloe laughed as she set the can on the table. "Stapler."

"That's one way to make an impression."

And didn't he say it would make him think of her for the rest of his life? "I just think city life has lost its luster. I miss the pace here. I miss Christmas festivities and Fourth of July down by the lake. There has to be more than busy city streets and people coming for your job."

"Do you think he's here to take you back?"

Chloe shrugged. "I'm nothing to him. Besides I have a job offer for after the first of the year. I just need to decide if I want something that big again."

"I've known you since we were little. You always had big aspirations." Melanie stood as the bell over the front door rang for the hundredth time that day. "Are you going to talk to him again?"

Nodding, Chloe picked up the can and took another sip. "I told him I'd have dinner with him tonight."

"That's a start. And just so you know, you have a secure job here for as long as you like. It's nice to have you around again. I missed you. But, you're also big city now, and I mean that in a good way. I think you'd tire from all of this the moment the holidays were over. Think about that."

What was left for her but to think about that?

She thought about heading home and changing before dinner, but that would only stir up conversations she wasn't ready to have with her mother. Maybe she'd stroll up and down Main Street and take in the evening sights, too.

* * *

JASON SAT at the small desk in his room at the Aubrey Heights Inn. It certainly had a cute, small town appeal. The lace drapes on the windows, the small rose print on the bedspread and the chair upholstery, and the antique dresser took a traveler back in time.

He could smell the scents from the small restaurant at the Inn, which he'd noticed only had ten tables at most. Because he was big city, he'd made sure to reserve one of those tables, just in case the town was overrun by hungry patrons at seven o'clock.

The glow from his laptop screen illuminated the room as the sun had tucked itself in early. For the first time in Jason's life, he sat there staring at the string of emails, not wanting to answer a single one.

Through adulthood, he'd been all business. He'd been in the business club in high school, followed with a bachelor's degree, and then a master's degree. There wasn't anything about business he didn't know —except how to walk away from it.

Advertising had always called to him. He'd been ten-years-old when he'd opened his first lemonade stand and learned the skillful maneuvering of marketing. He'd been eleven when he'd purchased that mountain bike everyone had their eye on. He'd been twelve when he'd replaced it because someone had stolen it. The one part of it all that stayed constant was that Jason Mitchell could sell anything with an ad campaign.

It had worked for him when he'd run for student council, and no bake sale or car wash had ever made more money. Oh, he'd always known he'd end up at the top of firm bringing in big accounts.

What he hadn't planned on was someone like Deborah King standing in his way and swatting him down. When he'd left *Stockton Advertising*, he thought things could only go upward. *Mason Arts* was where he was supposed to make his mark.

Now, he sat in a small hotel room contemplating his future.

Outside his window, the streetlights, decorated with wreaths and ribbons, illuminated the snow-covered street filled with tourists and locals soaking in the Christmas spirit. Every store was still open, and he was sure that was for the season as well. It had to be profitable enough to hire extra employees and bring in more stock.

Jason eased back in his chair. What could he offer the fine people of Aubrey Heights? They were already well known for their Christmas festivities. Could his talents make the following Christmas even more profitable for the citizens?

He stood and walked to the nightstand where there lay a brochure on the many wonders that Aubrey Heights offered all year round.

There was a lake hidden back in the hills about two miles where it looked as if the Fourth of July was a big hit with fireworks and festivities.

Starting in June, and running through September, there was a farmers' market just on the outskirts of town. A Harvest Festival filled the streets, according to the photos, in October. And he should have known that the Easter bunny would have an enormous egg hunt in the spring.

Perhaps Aubrey Heights was worth giving a chance.

Would Chloe be staying in town as well? That was the million-dollar question. What did she have left back in the city?

CHAPTER 25

*T*here had been some contemplation about not showing up. But, if Chloe Richardson was anything, she was true to her word. Not like others she'd worked with—William Mason for example.

She'd walked through the shops and lingered near the Christmas tree in the center of town to take in the ambiance.

In the past two weeks, she'd had many meals with Jason, but her stomach twisted and turned when she'd headed toward the Inn to have dinner with him.

She wasn't entirely sure what he was doing in Aubrey Heights. Of course, she hadn't given him much time to tell her either. All she knew was she wanted him gone. Having him that close to her seemed to be stirring up hurt feelings, and she didn't need that. The city had rejected her. She didn't need the city following her to her safe haven and rejecting her there too.

Walking up the front steps to the Inn filled Chloe with a joy she hadn't expected. The lights from inside bathed the wrap-around porch in warmth. Christmas lights hung from the gutters and twinkled as if they played to a silent song.

She could smell the aromas that floated from the kitchen before she even opened the door to the cozy inside.

Guests lingered in the formal living room, and the sound of dishes clinking, and conversation instantly filled her ears.

"I'm glad you made it." She heard Jason's voice behind her and turned to see him standing there. Other than gym clothes, she realized it was the first time she'd seen him look casual. Was he wearing jeans and a sweater that afternoon?

His dark hair fell over his brow, hiding the scar she'd given him when they'd met. And his eyes, they were a deeper shade of blue than she'd remembered.

Swallowing down the lump that had lodged in her throat, she forced a smile to her lips. "I told you I'd be here."

The smile that formed on his lips was gentle. "They have our table right inside, by the window."

Gesturing with his hand, he escorted her inside the dining room. Chloe nodded to those she knew and watched those she didn't know look up at her as she passed through. Small town. Everyone noticed everyone.

Jason pulled out her seat.

"Thank you," she said as she sat and he took the adjacent seat. "It smells delightful in here."

"They had cookies in the living room. I think I had six of them. If their suppers are as good, I'm never leaving."

Her breath caught in her lungs. He didn't mean that, she told herself as she laid her napkin in her lap. Aubrey Heights wasn't the kind of place for a corporate man.

A woman who had been into the store earlier that morning approached that table wearing a white frilly apron. She introduced herself, handed them each a small printed menu, and explained the dinner choices. They both chose the comfort of Shepherd's Pie, and Jason ordered them a bottle of wine. They sat in awkward silence as it was delivered and poured.

One glass wouldn't hurt, Chloe decided as she folded her hands in her lap beneath the table.

Jason lifted his glass of wine and held it toward her, cuing her to lift her glass. "Here's to a town filled with Christmas spirit like no other."

Chloe tapped her glass to his. "To Christmas spirit," she repeated before taking a sip.

She couldn't help but notice that as he drank, his eyes stayed on her. Was her hair a mess? Did she have something on her face?

"You look beautiful tonight," he said as he set his glass on the table.

"Why are you here?" she had to ask. If it was to ask her back, she didn't think she could go. If it was to tell her to stay away, he could have done that with an email.

Before he answered, he lifted his glass and took a long sip from his wine. "I needed to see you."

"If you came all this way to ask me to go back to the firm…"

"I didn't."

"Well, then if you want the inside information on Gloria Vandenberg…"

"I don't."

"You sure as hell didn't have a trip planned to come Christmas shopping."

Jason shrugged as the waitress came to the table with their dinner plates and set them down. "God, this looks delicious. I can't remember the last time I had this," he said digging his fork into the creamy potatoes. "Now I remember," he said with his mouth full, and his face showing the obvious signs of enjoyment—including his eyes closing. "My grandmother would make this. Damn, now I really miss her."

Chloe picked up her fork and took a bite. She'd had that meal at the Inn before. It was a tradition for New Year's, and she'd probably have it again when she came with her parents before the fireworks were set off, ringing in the new year.

What would a new year bring? A trip to Brazil and a new opportunity, she thought. Should she tell Jason about that? Why should she? He hadn't even told her what he was doing in Aubrey Heights.

EVERY BITE he took of his dinner made Jason miss his grandmother just a little more. Oh, he wasn't going to be some big sobbing baby, but he could admit to himself, at least, that he felt the tears choking him.

His grandmother lived in a small town not far from Aubrey Heights. He understood the appeal of knowing everyone and centering your life around traditions.

They had a large Christmas tree in that town too —nothing like in Aubrey Heights, but it was memorable.

Santa could always find him at his grandmother's house, and he thought that was extra special. The man was miraculous, and that had him chuckling.

"What's so funny?" Chloe asked.

"I was thinking about how smart Santa is."

Her brows drew together as she watched him devour his dinner.

"You don't still believe in Santa, do you?"

Jason picked up his wine and sipped. "Not since Cole Zimmerman spilled the beans in the fifth grade. What a jerk."

"Maybe he saved your life. You certainly didn't want to go into high school without knowing those specifics."

Jason laughed as he took another bite.

Perhaps she was loosening up. He'd seen that they were having carriage rides on the street. Maybe he could convince her to take one with him.

"Do you work tomorrow?" he asked as he eased back in his chair, his stomach full from the food he had shoveled in.

"Of course. Tomorrow is Wednesday and Melanie's store is in its Christmas rush."

"Right."

Chloe blotted her mouth with her napkin and her gaze fixed on him. "Do you work tomorrow?" she asked, and he could see the worry settle in her eyes.

"To tell you the truth, I'm fairly sure by tomorrow I won't have a job."

"They let you go too? Is that why you're here?"

Jason eased forward and rested his arms on the table. "I knew you didn't walk out. I just knew you wouldn't do that."

"That only explains why I left. I don't need to be where I'm not wanted."

Jason reached his hand across the table and covered hers. "And I don't want to be where you're not."

CHAPTER 26

Chloe sat there, rendered speechless. Jason's thumb brushed over her knuckles. Her breath stuck in her lungs and her heart hammered in her chest.

He'd left the city because she wasn't in it?

What was she supposed to do with that information?

When Jason moved his head, his hair parted so that she could see the scar that had formed on his forehead. She'd done that to him, and now here he was holding her hand and telling her he didn't want to be where she wasn't?

She needed to breathe. She needed a moment to collect her thoughts. She needed...

"Is there anything else I can get for you?" The waitress had returned to the table.

Jason, his hand still on Chloe's, looked up at the waitress. "I think we're going to need a few boxes to take home the rest of our dinner."

He was right. How could she even consider eating after that?

When the waitress had left, Jason leaned in, his eyes searching hers.

"Are you okay?"

Chloe shook her head. "No. Why did you say that?"

"That we needed boxes? Because you haven't taken any more bites and I'm so full that..."

"No. Why did you say you didn't want to be where I wasn't?"

His lips parted into a glorious smile that made her go lightheaded.

"Let's finish this conversation outside," he offered as he pulled his hand back from hers when the waitress delivered the foam boxes.

HE'D SPOOKED HER, though he hadn't meant to. In his opinion there just wasn't any reason not to put it out there. They didn't work together anymore, and that had been his rule—no dating co-workers. What continued to play in his mind was that embrace they had shared in his office. It hadn't been just a celebration—no it went much deeper than that. There were feelings between them, and he didn't want to chance losing his opportunity to share his thoughts on that. What if she was still in love with Tyler Ashby? Old flames could reignite. If he didn't take his chance now, he'd never get another one.

Should she turn him away, he could go back to the city and find a new job. He wasn't without opportunity. But in his heart, he didn't want to go back without her.

Jason paid the bill, picked up the box of food, and followed when Chloe stood and started for the door.

She struggled with her coat as they walked through the door and out onto the porch that surround the Inn. Jason lifted his hand to help her.

"I've got it," she snapped. Oh, yeah, he'd frazzled her.

"What do you say we take a walk around town? Maybe take a carriage ride?" he offered, but his suggestions were met with an icy stare.

"I don't understand why you're here. You're not here to ask me to come back to my job—and I won't come back. I will not work for people who don't appreciate me. And *Deb* can have my office, that's fine. I won't steal *Pop! Cosmetics* out from under you either."

Turning, Jason set the box of food on a nearby rocking chair and turned back to face her. "Do you think that's why I'm here?"

"I can't imagine any other reason than to either ask me back or ask me to stay away. And whatever that was about in there, that whole thing about you not wanting to be where I'm not—you're going to lose your job spending time here. I don't know why..."

He couldn't help but to shut her up in the only way that made sense to him, and perhaps get his point across to her.

Jason stepped in toward her, closing the gap between them, and caressing her cold cheek with his hand before he dipped his head to press his lips to hers.

He felt her stiffen beneath his touch, and he braced for her punch, but it never came.

A moment later her lips softened against his and then opened to accept his kiss. Lifting her hands, she pressed them to his chest, and only because he had on his thick coat, he knew she couldn't feel his heart pounding.

Jason slipped his other arm around her waist and pulled her in closer so that their bodies were pressed together. This was what he'd wanted since the moment he'd walked into her office and introduced himself. This was the brass ring—the winning sales pitch.

He didn't care about advertising at that moment, clients, or even the fact that *Deb* would make sure he never worked in the industry again. All he could think about was how warm Chloe made him feel, even as the cold bit at his skin.

As he pulled back, wondering what her reaction was going to be, he watched as her eyes remained closed for a moment before they fluttered open and stared into his.

"You kissed me," she said, and the cold carried her breath away in a cloud.

"I did. And you kissed me back."

"I did." Still her voice was light and airy. "Why did you kiss me?"

"Because I can't stop thinking about you. I've wanted to kiss you since the day I walked into your office."

"They day you took my job," she reminded him, and suddenly her voice wasn't as soft.

"I didn't know that. I never would have taken it if I'd known..." This time she cut off his words by moving in and kissing him.

But this time the kiss wasn't sweet and warm. There was a fury to it, perhaps even some anger as he wrapped his arms around her, and she draped herself around his neck.

People walked in and out of the Inn, and he'd heard someone whistle, but he couldn't break free. There was nowhere he wanted to be more than in her arms with her mouth pressed against his. Was this love? Was this guilt? He'd never felt anything like it before. He'd only met Chloe a few weeks ago, but he'd walked away from the job that meant more to him than anything just to be in this moment. It was worth it—of this he was sure.

She was breathless when she pulled away, and she gripped the lapels of his coat. "I can't do this. I can't fall into this."

"Into what?"

"Whatever this is. I can't start over with you here."

She hadn't let go yet, and he wasn't going to let her take off—not yet.

"Don't make that decision right now. Chloe, I want to be with you. I want to be with you enough that I rented a car and drove six hours just hoping I'd have a moment like this. I have no other motives than wanting to be with you."

Her eyes were searching his, but for what? Truth? He was speaking it.

"I have to go home." Now Chloe turned, but he caught her wrist and stopped her from heading down the steps.

"Stay with me, Chloe."

She shook her head. "I can't. My heart was already broken once this week. I can't let it happen again."

And with those final words, she turned and headed into the falling snow, disappearing under the shimmer of the streetlamp.

CHAPTER 27

*S*leep didn't come. Chloe paced her small bedroom still painted pink with little roses on the wall. She walked in and out of the adjoining bathroom, flipping on and off the light.

Quietly she had made three trips up and down the stairs, pacing the house trying to clear her mind.

Jason Mitchell had left the city and come looking for her. What kind of madman did that? He walked away from the account she brought the firm. The account she thought he would take care of when she left. Of course, she hadn't intended on leaving.

She stood at the sink and looked out into the darkness through the window. She hadn't anticipated wandering around her parents' home in the middle of the night, dreading getting up to go work retail at Christmas time. God, she'd avoided retail at Christmas time like the plague when she was younger. Now, it was her escape.

Quietly, Chloe walked back up the stairs into her bedroom, closing the door behind her. Across the room, she noticed that her cell phone had lit up. Walking to it, she noticed there was a text message.

It was from Tyler Ashby.

I've had some schedule changes this week, so I'm heading to Aubrey Heights. Can we meet?

It was three o'clock in the morning. What was he doing texting her?

I look forward to seeing you, she texted back.

Chloe turned off her phone and crawled back into bed. She had to keep reminding herself that the new year was bringing her new opportunity. So, she wouldn't be catering to the every whim of a furniture heiress running a cosmetic company, but if she took Tyler's job offer, she'd be part of something bigger.

All she had to do was keep her focus.

But as her head hit the pillow, she was reminded of the reason she been pacing the house all night. Jason Mitchell was in town, and he'd kissed her. He'd kissed her senseless. Was that a Christmas miracle or Christmas disaster? She had no idea.

Chloe turned to her side and pulled the comforter up over her head. The only certain thing she knew was that if she didn't get any sleep, she was going to have a horrible day at work. And even in a place like Aubrey Heights, dealing with the general public at Christmas time needed all your attention.

* * *

JASON HAD BOUNDED down the stairs by seven o'clock. The aroma of brewing coffee and baked goods had stirred him from a restless night of sleep.

As he entered the dining room and picked up a cup to fill with coffee from the carafe, he thought about the day ahead.

Stirring sugar into his coffee, and picking up a croissant, he sat down at the table he and Chloe had occupied the night before. The thought of her had kept him from a good night's sleep. She hadn't seemed very happy to see him, and that was disappointing. He wasn't sure what he had expected, but he had hoped she would have been a little more excited.

Then he thought of the kiss. There was a fluttering in his chest when it came to his mind. He had thought of kissing her the day he met her, perhaps he should have. What would have happened had he moved on that instinct weeks ago? He still would've had a scar on his forehead, he humored himself. He thought of her sitting in the emergency room filling out papers for him, what if he had kissed her then? Would things have been completely different? Would they both still be in the city? Or, would they both have been dismissed?

He took his first bite of the buttery croissant and wiped his mouth with a napkin that was arranged on the table. He hadn't opened his computer during the long hours of last night. It was a good chance that buried in his inbox was a release of his position. And if there wasn't one, he wasn't so sure he wouldn't write one himself.

Jason hadn't come to Aubrey Heights to beg Chloe back to work. No, in fact he had resigned to the fact that he would be fired for his actions. The only reason he had driven six hours in a rental car was to see her face. He wasn't going to leave Aubrey Heights without her in tow. And, if that meant he lived in Aubrey Heights the rest of his life, well, it seemed like a nice place to live.

He chuckled to himself as he lifted his coffee cup to his lips. Driving to Chloe's hometown, and surprising her at work had been the most spontaneous thing he had ever done. The kiss he planted on her, the night before on the porch, was equally, splendidly spontaneous.

Never in his entire life had he ever felt this way about anyone. He never would've chased any other woman down. Did that make him creepy? Was he some kind of stalker?

No, the fluttering he felt in his chest told him it was something different. He had fallen in love with the woman.

He set down his cup of coffee and pushed away the plate with the croissant. Dear God, he was in love with her.

Repeating it again and again in his mind seemed to only make him more lightheaded. What was he going to do about that? Sure, she had kissed him back last night, but she didn't accept his invitation to stay with him.

Jason ran his hand over his cheek and realized he had forgotten to shave. He wasn't going back up to do it. He had some thinking to do. If he blurted out the words *I love you*, would she run the other direction? If a woman did that to him, after only a few weeks of knowing him, he probably would run the other direction, too. Hell, she'd already thrown a stapler at his head. Perhaps he should mention it to her when they weren't at the quaint little store she worked at. He would hate to see her destroy anything by throwing it at him.

Perhaps he could find a moment with Chloe's boss. Maybe she could help him coordinate a time to get Chloe out of the store. Ideas began to explode in his brain. He was in one of the most romantic settings he'd ever seen. The snow. The cold. The scenery. Christmas sights and scents. It all surrounded them, and who wouldn't be pulled in by its charm?

Jason lifted his head as the front door to the Inn opened, and a man and a woman were greeted by the innkeeper. What a unique place Chloe Richardson came from. People with packed bags flooded to the small town to take in its magic. Sure, they did that in the city too, but no one noticed. Here, people noticed when someone else arrived in town.

Was Chloe immune to its magic? Or could he use it to his advantage? Was there enough magic left in Aubrey Heights to convince her to spend the rest of her life with him?

CHAPTER 28

With Christmas only one week away, Chloe was happy to see the store packed with people. She had hoped to be distracted so that she wouldn't think about her dinner date last night, or the kiss that followed after. It was nearing her lunch break, and she hadn't seen Jason walk into the store. He hadn't texted her or called her. Perhaps he went home.

That thought had her head spinning. Did she want him to go home? Did she want him to return to the city and the life that he knew? Did she want to return to that?

Chloe was busy restocking the candle section when the door to the shop open for the hundredth time. There was no need to look up, as Melanie swiftly moved to the new customer and welcomed them. It was only then she heard a high-pitched voice of the cosmetics diva.

Chloe looked up to see Gloria Vandenberg, dressed in what she considered a ridiculous outfit, running toward her in stilettos.

"Oh my God, Chloe. Is this the cutest store? And this little town," she tossed her hands in the air and the bracelets on her wrist clinked together, "it's like a *Hallmark* movie."

Setting the candle she was holding down on the shelf, Chloe tucked her hands into the pockets of her apron. "Gloria, what are you doing here?"

"What am I doing here? What are you doing here?"

Chloe focused on keeping the smile on her face. "I was let go. At this time a year, the only logical thing was to come home. So here I am."

Gloria leaned in toward her. "This is not where you belong. I hired you to take care of my advertising."

"And they fired me," Chloe said, and knew the smile had slipped from her lips.

"And that is why I fired them."

Chloe took a step back, her eyes now focused on the teal-painted lids of Gloria's eyes. "You fired them?"

"That *Deb* is a piece of work." Gloria crossed her arms in front of her. "She moved in as if she were my best friend. And that morning I hired you, that was glorious."

Gloria looked down at her claw-shaped finger-nails and examined them.

"I've never seen anyone lose their temper quite like that," Gloria chuckled at the memory. "So you can guarantee when I showed up for that meeting, and William Mason had the nerve to tell me that you had been let go, and *Deb* was sitting at the table," Gloria threw her hands up in the air, "I let them have it."

Chloe pressed her fingers to her lips to keep from laughing out loud. "You left the firm over me?"

"I most certainly did. You're my girl."

"Well, I don't have anything to offer you right now. I don't even have a job other than this one."

Gloria gathered Chloe's hands in hers and held them tightly. "Like hell you don't. I want you to run the advertising department for *Pop! Cosmetics.*"

The breath in Chloe's lungs whooshed out and caused her to go a bit lightheaded. "You want me to run your advertising department?"

"Yes. I don't make decisions lightly."

"No, no you don't. But I have to tell you, I have another offer."

Gloria let go of Chloe's hands and took a step back. "I'll pay you double."

Chloe laughed. "I haven't even negotiated that part yet."

Gloria lifted one of her manicured fingers. "Ah, then you really haven't taken the job yet have you?"

"What job is that?" Jason's voice came from behind the candle display, and Chloe watched as he walked toward them.

"How long have you been there? I thought maybe you left town," Chloe said and noticed that Gloria's attention had shifted toward Jason.

"I'm not done here quite yet," he said as he now turned his attention to Gloria. "Jason Mitchell," he offered, extending his hand toward Gloria.

"Jason Mitchell? Your name was on all those documents I tore up at that meeting the other day."

Chloe saw the humor of dance in Jason's eyes. "That was a mighty bold move," he said. "I heard all about the meeting."

Gloria pulled her hand back and pressed it to her chest. "I've always been told I'm a little bit dramatic."

To that, Jason laughed. "I think it added just the right touch. I wish I could have given them the same reaction when they fired me."

Chloe turned to him. "They fired you? They fired you because you came here? You have to go back. You can't throw that all away because you came here."

The humor was still fresh in his eyes, and he smiled at her which made her heart thump a little harder. "I told you I didn't want to be there without you."

"Be where without you?" Chloe turned when she heard Tyler Ashby's voice behind her.

His arm slipped around her waist, and he kissed her on the cheek. "It sounds like these people are trying to steal you away from me," Tyler humored before extending his hand to shake Jason's. "Tyler Ashby."

Chloe watched the humor disappear from Jason's eyes and a flash of irritation replaced it. "Jason Mitchell."

Tyler shook his hand, and then turned his attention to Gloria. Extending his hand to her, he said, "And you are?"

"Gloria Vandenberg," she said as she raised her jaw. "*Pop! Cosmetics.*"

"Vandenberg," Tyler repeated. "I think our families were neighbors in the Hamptons."

Chloe watched as Gloria's attitude eased into friendly. "Ashby. I do think I recognize the name."

Tyler turned his attention back to Chloe, and taking both of her hands, he smiled at her. "When is your lunch break? I want to discuss our plans."

Chloe's throat went dry. She could feel the other two sets of eyes watching her every move. "I don't know when I can get away," she said.

"She's ready to go now," Melanie called out across the store.

When Chloe lifted her eyes to Melanie to send her a scowl, Melanie laughed and gave her a sign to leave. Perhaps it wasn't that she was setting her up, maybe the scene was causing problems. It sure was causing problems for Chloe.

Tyler gave her hand a squeeze. "Let's have lunch at the Inn. I'll meet you over there."

Just as Chloe took a breath to reject his invitation, she noticed Jason taking a step toward Tyler. "I saw you walk into the Inn this morning. You were escorted to your room with a woman."

"I most certainly was. It's a beautiful place isn't it? The Inn and this town. And to think I have both of my girls here." He turned and kissed Chloe on the cheek again. "I'll meet you there. I'll get us a table."

All three of them watched as Tyler walked to the door, giving Melanie a wave, before he walked out to the street.

"*Girl!* What are you into?" Gloria laughed. "You have a man who keeps two women? And then you got this one vying for your attention?" She tipped her head toward Jason. "No wonder you're not taking my proposal seriously."

"I am taking your proposal seriously," Chloe stammered as her hands shook. "I'm just a little surprised by it."

Gloria chuckled. "I'm going to go shopping. I want to see what this little town is all about. Maybe I'll go sit on Santa's lap." Gloria looked down at her phone, which was pink and blinged out with diamonds. "I have a meeting online at two. Why don't you and I meet at that cute little coffee shop at four and discuss your options."

There was no time to confirm or reject the invitation. Gloria turned and left the store leaving Chloe and Jason standing alone.

"So that was Tyler Ashby, huh?" He asked jamming his hands into the pockets of his coat.

"Yes, but what does that..."

"Well, it looks like you already have a man in your life. I'm not sure you're the only woman in his."

Chloe took a breath to explain the situation, but Jason quickly interrupted.

"I had hoped to spend Christmas here with you. It's quite a magical place. But, now that I'm unemployed, I guess maybe I'll go visit my mother in Florida."

"Jason..."

He held up his hand. "I was a fool to come here. I let my head and my heart get away from me. I will always be grateful for having known you," he said as he stepped in and kissed her on the cheek.

Chloe watched as he turned and left the store. Now she stood alone in the space where chaos had surrounded her. What had just happened? Jason had come for her. Gloria had offered her a job. And Tyler had swooped in, stirred it all up, and walked out the door.

"Are you going to get out of here or not?" Melanie called out across the store. "I don't know what's going on, but I can't focus if I'm concentrating on all the drama you're bringing in here," she laughed. "Go. Go get that man. And go secure one of those jobs. Your bigger than Aubrey Heights, Chloe. Now go."

CHAPTER 29

*C*hloe didn't even think to get her coat. Instead, she ran out the door of the shop and onto the sidewalk where the sun had tucked itself away behind snow clouds that began to cover the streets with snow again.

She shivered as she looked for Jason, but he had disappeared in the wall of snow and people who hurried to escape it.

He'd be at the Inn, she was certain of that. Even if he was going there to pack and leave, she still had time to find him.

Her teeth chattered as she ran down the street toward the Inn. Wet strands of hair clung to her face, and her hands were numb from the cold that had begun whipping around her.

In the gray darkness of the storm, the lights to the Inn were welcoming.

She hurried up the walk pushed open the door as Tyler and Gwendolyn were walking down the steps.

"Chloe!" Tyler ran to her and pulled her inside. "What in the hell are you doing? Where's your coat? It's snowing outside and below freezing. You're soaking wet." His hands were on her arms, and her vision took a moment to focus on his face having gone from cold to warm.

"I'll go get her a towel," Gwendolyn said as she hurried back up the steps.

Tyler rubbed his hands up and down her arms. "You could have gotten frostbite. You know better than to be out in this. It's getting bad. They say we have at least ten inches coming."

She heard the words, but the blood rushing in her ears was louder.

Tyler pulled her to him to keep her warm. "You're a wonder, my Chloe." He laughed as his hands rubbed over her back. "I can't wait to have you in Brazil with us."

Chloe smelled his cologne before she saw him. Jason stood on the stairs, his suitcase in his hand. She turned to him. There was something very important she needed him to hear, but he shook his head and walked past them.

"Jason," she called after him, Tyler's hands still on her arms.

"You'll freeze to death out there. Take my coat," he said pulling it from his arms.

"I'm going to miss him."

"Where's he going to go? There is no car parked there, and his is under snow. Put on the damn coat," he demanded as he handed it to her.

Chloe pushed her arms through and shrugged on the heavy coat as Gwendolyn hurried down the stairs.

"I got the..." she began, but Tyler moved to her as Chloe hurried for the door.

IT HAD BEEN a stupid move on his part to chase her down to the small town she called home, but Jason couldn't have stopped himself once he'd realized what he'd felt. Even though there had been the chance he'd be disappointed, he hadn't considered being heartbroken.

The rental car, parked in the lot, was covered in snow. One thing was for sure, he wasn't going to be making a speedy exit from Aubrey Heights.

He unlocked the door and opened it. Throwing in his suitcase, he then found the brush to clean off the windshield when he heard his name being called from the Inn.

When he lifted his head, he saw Chloe running toward him in the coat he'd seen on Tyler.

"Go back inside, Chloe. It's freezing out here," he called back to her.

"Stop. I need to talk to you."

"I think your actions said enough. I'm the one in the wrong for being here. Just let me get the car…"

He turned from brushing snow off the windshield and she was standing next to him. Her hair was wet, cheeks bright red, and her breath carried on the frozen air.

"You're going to catch something standing out here like that," he scolded.

"I'm here to catch something," she panted as she spoke. "I'm here to catch you."

"I think your dance card is full. Why don't you go back inside…"

"What are you talking about? Why are you so mad?"

Jason set the brush on the hood of the car, and took the scarf from around his neck, and covered Chloe's head. He'd feel even worse if she got pneumonia. "I'm not mad," he decided. "I just need to go. I don't belong here with you and Tyler, and that other woman. You're going to get hurt, Chloe. That's all I'm going to say about that."

He reached for the brush and she gripped his wrist in her frozen hand. "That other woman? Gwendolyn?"

"Well, I didn't get acquainted."

A small laugh broke through her mad. "That's Tyler's wife. They're newlyweds."

"And he's taking *you* to Brazil?"

"They're taking me with them to look at a coffee bean plantation for his company. He offered me a job, Jason."

Jason let out a breath, dissipating his own anger, and took Chloe's hands, holding them between his gloved ones. It wasn't like him to not assess a situation fully. This was a sure sign he'd let his heart do all the thinking and not his brain. Not since junior high school had he stood in front of a girl and felt like such a loser.

"Tyler offered you a job in his company? That's why you're going to Brazil?"

She smiled and he saw her lips quiver in the cold. "He pulled his contract with the agency when I told him they fired me. He offered me the position and yes, he invited me to go to Brazil, to see where they do business. I'd be working in the city, I suppose, at their headquarters. We haven't really hashed out the details. That's why he's here." She looked at her hands which he now had pressed to his chest. "And now I guess I have a job offer with Gloria, too."

"It looks like things panned out for you." How could he not be happy about that? He was the one losing out, and that was all on him.

"Not everything panned out," she lifted her eyes to meet his. "I figured something out in all of this, and those jobs don't mean anything without this other part working."

Jason lifted his gloved hand to her cheek and pushed the wet hair from her skin. "What did you figure out?"

"That I don't want to do any of this without you."

He chuckled. "Well, I could use a job."

Chloe shook her head. "No, not that. Well, maybe that." Her eyes shifted as if what he'd said added another layer to her manic state. "No, what I figured out was I don't want to do any of this without you. I want you in my life, Jason. I want you around me every day."

"What are you trying to say?"

She let out a breath that lingered on the frozen air and stepped in closer to him until their bodies were nearly pressed together.

"I'm saying that in all of this, I realized I love you."

Surely the pounding in his chest could be heard by everyone in town. Wasn't that exactly what he'd hoped she'd realized? He'd realized it the moment he'd kissed her, though he'd been fairly sure that was what had kept him up nights since the moment they'd met.

"You love me?"

She nodded. "I don't expect you to..."

He pulled her in, wrapping his arms around her waist, and she raised hers around his neck. Her blue eyes sparkled as she gazed up at him. "I love you, too. Of course I love you. Why would I have come here at the risk of losing everything if I didn't love you?"

"You love me?"

"Yeah, and apparently you love me."

"Are we crazy? We haven't known each other very long and..."

"And you put a scar on my heart just as you did my head."

She let out a laugh and traced her fingers over the scar on his forehead. "I'm sorry about that."

"I'm not. Just think, if you hadn't had to spend all that time with me in the emergency room, you'd just still be mad at me."

Chloe rested her head against his chest. "I don't think I was ever mad at you. You took my breath away when you first stepped into my office."

Jason pulled back so that she had to look up at him. "I did?"

The smile she flashed was beautiful. "I didn't want to leave you, but I had to come here."

"I think you need to stay here."

A crease formed between her brows. "What does that mean?"

"It means that you have a lot of opportunity coming your way, and Aubrey Heights suits you better than the city. Maybe you should think of starting your own firm and handling Tyler's marketing and Gloria's as well."

"From here?"

"Yes."

"I can't do that alone. It's too much. Those are huge companies and I..."

He rested his hand on her cheek to draw her attention back to him. "You wouldn't do it alone. I'd be here with you."

"You'd move to Aubrey Heights to work with me?"

"To be with you. What do you say? Stay here with me forever?"

"Forever?" Her voice trembled when she said the word.

"Forever, Chloe. As in, come to Florida with me, meet my mom, spend Christmas in my arms, go to

Brazil, open your own company, and spend forever with me. Marry me and settle here, right where you grew up."

Now he couldn't read her expression. It was possible he'd just stepped over that line again and he'd be the one sorry for it.

"Chloe!" Tyler's voice rang through the curtain of snow before they saw him walking toward them. "Is everything okay?"

She looked up into Jason's eyes again, and this time the smile brightened her entire face. "Everything's perfect. In fact, I'm getting married."

CHAPTER 30

*I*n all the years Chloe had lived in Aubrey Heights, and the many more that she'd been a visitor, she'd never been in one of the quaint rooms at the Inn.

Jason had run her a warm bath in the claw-foot tub, and Gwendolyn had brought her a change of clothes to borrow. As she soaked in the fragrant water of lavender, she considered what had happened in the parking lot.

She was engaged to a man she hardly knew, had only kissed, and loved more than anyone she'd ever loved in her life. Everything inside of her told her that the moment was right. It was the right time to move back. It was the right time to start her own marketing firm. It was the right time to fall in love with a man who had given up everything just to follow her.

What was her mother going to say? Her father would be livid. She hadn't brought Jason home to meet them. What kind of man proposes without a father's consent? Maybe that was old-fashioned, but that was how her father was.

It was only then that she realized the bath water

had started to go cold. She'd soaked away the chill long enough.

She'd promised them all to meet them in the lounge when she was done. Perhaps she'd made too many decisions too quickly. Would Jason understand if she changed her mind, or at least put some things on hold? Would he think she was having second thoughts? Was she?

No. She did love him. She felt that in her very core. Time. They needed time.

Chloe stepped out of the tub and pulled on the thick cotton robe that hung on the back of the door. Perhaps they could honeymoon at the Inn, she thought and remembered she was going to let that simmer. They might love each other, but nothing had to be rushed.

She took her time to dress in Gwendolyn's clothes and to dry her hair. She wished she had some makeup in her purse.

It was nearly an hour later that she descended the stairs at the Inn. She hadn't even thought about calling Melanie and telling her she wasn't coming back. Guilt sickened her, but maybe Melanie would understand.

She could hear the many conversations coming from the lounge and wondered how many people were staying there. Of course it would be filled with tourists. Everyone made their trek to Aubrey Heights at Christmas time. It was magical.

When she reached the last step, she heard the distinct laughter of her father. Her father?

She turned the corner to see the lounge filled with people she knew. Melanie was there, and why was she there? The store should be packed with shoppers. Gloria was there in an outfit that screamed high-priced ski vacation. Gwendolyn and

Tyler sat on the sofa next to her aunt Janice and cousin Roz.

In the corner of the room stood her parents with Jason, each with a flute of champagne in their hands.

Jason smiled when she entered the room and moved to her, handing her a flute and pressing a warm kiss to her lips in front of everyone, who had gone quiet.

"You look beautiful," he said softly.

"What's going on?" she whispered.

Sliding an arm around her waist he turned to look at the room full of people that Chloe loved. "They all came to celebrate with us. Your parents brought your aunt and cousin. Melanie closed the store because the snow has frightened away the tourists. Gloria has extended her stay, and Tyler and Gwendolyn are staying here, so that worked out well," he laughed.

"You told them all?" she whispered again.

Her father handed his glass to her mother and walked across the room toward her. "Nice young man you have here, Chloe."

"Dad…"

He pressed his finger to her lips. "He came out to the house this morning and introduced himself. Did you really throw a stapler at his head?"

Chloe chuckled as she looked at the scar she'd left. "Yes."

"He must really love you to put up with that," her father laughed. "I knew when I met him that he loved you. You just know after so many years of loving someone when a man falls in love with a woman. I've given him my blessing to marry you, and now I'm giving you my blessing to marry him and be as happy as your mother and I are."

The tears were automatic, and Chloe wrapped her

arms around her father's neck and absorbed the embrace he gave her. He was the first man she'd loved, because he knew how to love and how to show it.

"I love you, Daddy."

"I know. And I know you're going to be very happy," he said as he pulled back and wiped the tears from Chloe's cheeks. "All I want is for you to be happy."

"I am."

Jason slipped his arm around her waist again. "My mother will be here tomorrow if the snow lets up."

"She's flying here?"

"She's ecstatic that I found the love of my life and she can't wait to meet you."

"Oh, this is all so sudden." Chloe felt the magnitude of it choking her.

"You're not having second thoughts, are you?"

"No. No." She let out a sigh. "None of this was what I expected when I woke up this morning. It's a lot to take in."

Jason shifted a look to those who had gathered in the room, and then took Chloe's hand and walked toward the entry way. "I didn't mean to overwhelm you. And I'm sorry I told your parents."

Chloe rested her head against his chest. "I think it's sweet."

"Good. Your mother would like us to get married on Christmas. She thinks it would be magical."

Chloe laughed as she pulled back to look into the eyes of the man she loved. "Oh, the wedding she could plan in a year," she humored.

Jason shook his head. "I think she was thinking next week."

"This Christmas?"

"Yes."

"I don't— We're not— Really?"

Jason lifted his hand to her cheek, and she realized she could drown in the sea of blue in his eyes. "I have all I need. I'd be honored to marry you next week. But I can wait as long as you want. I just want to be with you, forever. I love you."

Chloe reached for his hand that lingered on her cheek and wrapped her fingers around his. "I love you. I would marry you today."

He pulled her in, and she inhaled the scent of him.

"Let's get married on Christmas then, surrounded by the important people in our life. Maybe I can talk Tyler into letting me join you all in Brazil. It'll be a honeymoon."

"I can't believe all of this is happening."

"Christmas miracle?"

She laughed. "I think it is."

CHAPTER 31

*J*t was unimaginable, Chloe thought as her mother and aunt fussed over the simple dress she had picked out at the bridal store. It wasn't fancy, but Chloe wasn't interested in fancy. In fact, the dress, cake, flowers, and DJ were all fluff pieces her mother and aunt wanted for her wedding. As far as Chloe was concerned, she'd be happy to marry Jason at the courthouse and celebrate with dinner at the Inn after.

Jason, on the other hand, seemed to enjoy spending money on the event.

His mother had arrived two days after they'd decided to get married, and Chloe found that she was very fond of her. She could see where his mother would fuss over him, and perhaps he was in need of that as well. After all, everyone in town had rallied to get Chloe ready for her big day.

Her big day, she thought again. In all of her life, she hadn't been that little girl who thought about her wedding day, or who she would marry. She was too practical for that.

No, she'd always been busy promoting the latest lemonade or hot chocolate stand that she and her friends had built. There was always something to create for herself, a future with a man hadn't been on her radar.

The moment she'd met Jason, when she'd choked on her cold coffee and he swooped in with that bottle of water, she'd known something was different. She thought she'd just been consumed by his looks, but maybe it was more. Maybe fate came with a zap of electricity—which was what she felt when she saw him that day.

"We'd better get you out of this. Jason is headed over for dinner, and we can't have him seeing you in the dress before the wedding," her mother directed as she fixed the final pin into the hem of the dress.

"I don't see where it would matter. There is nothing traditional about this wedding," Chloe said as she looked at herself in the mirror.

"You look traditional. And his expression is what will matter. I've seen how he looks at you, but when he sees you in this dress, that moment will be price-less." Her mother stood behind her and rested her hands on Chloe's shoulders. As they both studied the mirror, Chloe realized how much she resembled her mother, whom she'd always thought was such a beau-tiful woman.

"You know Dad still looks at you the same way Jason looks at me."

"And aren't I a lucky woman too?"

* * *

JASON HAD JOINED them for dinner, and now Chloe was comfortably resting in his arms in his bed at the Inn. Would their life always be so spontaneous? She hadn't taken Jason to be that way when she'd met him. No, she figured he was power hungry and ruthless. No, she thought again, that was only after she'd realized William Mason had cut her out of her job. She couldn't have been more wrong about Jason. Something had told her, the first time she peered into those blue eyes, that there was kindness in his soul. She was truly happy that she hadn't run him off by throwing the stapler at him

"What are you thinking?" he asked as he brushed his fingers over her forehead moving the strands of hair that had fallen over her brow.

"That I had you pegged all wrong. When I met you, I thought you were sexy, but ruthless."

He chuckled. "Why would you think that?"

"Because you took my job."

"Hmmm," he made the noise and pressed a kiss to her head. "I never meant to."

"But I didn't know that. And now, here we are, only a few weeks later. We're getting married and sleeping in the bed we just made love in, while Christmas lights twinkle outside the window."

"That sounds like a Christmas fairy tale."

"It does, doesn't it?" Chloe propped herself up on her elbow. "I'm afraid that once midnight strikes on New Year's it'll all go away. Just like Cinderella's gown and carriage."

"Would you like to wait to get married?" he offered.

Chloe let out a breath and settled back in next to him, nuzzling her cheek to his chest. "No. I don't even want to wait one more day."

"It'll be worth it. I promise. And then, we'll start our own empire, right here in Aubrey Heights."

"You'll stay here? Live here? For real?"

"Chloe, haven't you figured it out yet? I love you and you're all I need. Besides, imagine bringing your clients here to stay at the Inn. Wouldn't this wow them too?"

"More than a suite at the Plaza?"

"Way more. So much more personal."

"I'm worried that I won't get clients."

He shifted to look at her. "You already have the two biggest clients you brought to the firm. What more do you need?"

Chloe laughed. "This is the part that you don't understand about me yet, because you haven't really seen me work. I'm always looking for the next client. I want a team, Jason. I want to run all the advertising campaigns in the world."

Jason laughed, and rolled Chloe atop of him. "You have vision."

"I worked hard for it."

"You did, and you'll be as big as *Mason Arts* if not bigger."

The thought thrilled her and gave her hope. But then she thought of Byron being pushed out by his own son. "I'm sad for Byron Mason though. I truly don't think he would have wanted to lose us over this."

"It's not personal, Chloe. It was all a business decision. You can't expect him to not side with his son."

"And you'll be my partner?"

Jason caressed her face with his hand. "Forever."

With her heart filled with love for the man, she pressed a kiss to the scar over his eye, and then one to his lips. "I love you, Mr. Mitchell."

"I love you, too, soon-to-be Mrs. Mitchell."

CHAPTER 32

Chloe woke to the aroma of coffee and food being cooked in the restaurant of the Inn. It was delightful.

When she rolled over, the bed was empty and Jason's side cold. The door to the bathroom was open and the light was off. She sat up and looked around. Jason was gone.

Certainly he hadn't left for good, the thought crossed her mind as her eyes darted toward the armoire where his suitcase rested on the shelf and his shirts hung. No, he hadn't left for good.

Her heart settled. She supposed until they were married for a while, she'd wonder if there would be a time when he would disappear in the middle of the night—forever. Did people who had known each other for years before marriage have that fear too?

A moment later the door opened, and Jason hurried in with a cup of coffee in each hand. He was showered and dressed as if he were going to a business meeting.

"Where were you?" Chloe asked as she sat up in bed and pulled the sheet to cover herself from anyone who might walk by.

Jason kicked the door closed with his foot. "I had a text message this morning, early. I'm going back downstairs. Take your shower and get dressed and meet me down there," he demanded.

Panic surged through her. "What's going on?"

Jason set one of the coffee mugs on the nightstand and then let out a long breath. "Just hurry." With his free hand he raked his fingers through his hair. "Yeah, just hurry."

He turned, still holding his own cup of coffee in his hand and walked out the door.

Chloe sat there for another long moment wondering what had stirred him up. Had she gotten into his head about the wedding and her nerves? What if he bailed on marrying her? What if he changed his mind?

Seriously, she needed to stop thinking like that. What kind of marriage started with doubt like that?

Chloe hurried through her shower, tied her hair back in a tail, and threw on the dress she'd brought with her so they could eat in town.

With a swipe of the mascara wand and a touch of lipstick, she was ready to face her fiancé and whatever had made him so manic.

Jason sat at the table tapping his spoon against the bottom of his coffee cup. Byron Mason chuckled from across the table as he sipped from his own cup. Tyler watched him carefully, and that too made him nervous.

He could sense her before she even walked through the door. Jason lifted his head to see his bride-to-be hurry into the restaurant and stop when she saw the company he was keeping. Before she could even speak, Gloria floated in through the front door in an obnoxious fur coat and scooped her up in a hug.

"It's not real fur," he heard her say to Chloe. "But I couldn't pass it up. This town is so freaking cute."

Both women turned their attention back to the table where Jason sat with the other men.

"Oh, good. You're all here," Gloria said as she took Chloe's arm and led her toward the table.

Jason stood, kissed Chloe on the cheek, and pulled a chair out for her as Byron did the same for Gloria.

"What's all this?" Chloe asked as the waitress brought two cups of coffee over for the women who had joined the table. "Byron, it's nice to see you."

Byron reached across the table for Chloe's hand, and patted it with his other. "Sweetheart, it's good to see you too. You look happy. You're glowing."

"Oh," she sighed and shifted a glance to Jason, before turning her attention back to Byron Mason. "Thank you."

Byron sat back in his chair, crossing one leg over the other. "I didn't even think you two liked each other." Jason chuckled and Chloe shifted a horrified glance his way. "It was quite a shock to find out you were getting married. Nearly as much of a shock to find out you didn't resign, but that my son had pushed you out of my company."

Chloe had lifted her cup to take a sip, but stopped. "Mr. Mason," she began, but Byron held up his hand to stop her.

"We all make mistakes, darling. Mine was hiring my son. He's manipulative and vindictive. He did bring in Jason, and that seems to have panned out for you, but I had never intended on losing you. That position was yours, and I let him undermine my decision on that. For that I'm truly sorry."

Jason took Chloe's hand. "Mr. Mason has come here to discuss business with you." He shifted his glance to the others at the table. "With all of you."

Gloria threw up her hands. "I said I wouldn't work with your company after what you did to Chloe."

"I don't blame you," Mason agreed, resting a hand on Gloria's. "That's why I'm here." He shifted his gaze back to Chloe. "I fired my son and that woman he brought in from that other agency. He didn't have my best interest in mind, or anyone else's. Instead, I came here to talk business with you. Only I find that Jason is here, you're getting married, and two of the biggest clients you brought to the firm are here too. I've come to ask you to come back. I'd like to make you a partner at the agency and someday sell it to you."

Chloe's mouth opened, but words never surfaced.

Jason gave her hand a squeeze. "Before you came down, I told him we'd like to buy his company out-right. He deserves a retirement." He smiled at the woman he loved who seemed to be at a loss for words.

"I can't afford that," she said softly. "Mr. Mason, that's very generous, but…"

"I'll pitch in," Tyler said, sitting up in his chair and leaning in toward the table. "Business is good, and that has a lot to do with you, sweetheart. You're ge-nius at what you do."

"I'm in," Gloria chimed in with a raise of her hand, a pointed fingernail painted bright pink making a statement. "Girl, you know your business, and I want you working with me. I'd go with you solo or in a big firm. But you deserve this. What they did to you was wrong. And this makes it all feel right."

Chloe pressed her hand to her mouth and leaned in toward Jason. "I don't know what to say."

"Say yes, to all of it. We can have a staff here and one in the city. Best of both worlds, sweetheart."

Tyler propped his elbows on the table to get closer to Chloe. "I have it under good authority that the coffee house will be upgraded."

"Why?"

"I bought it," he informed her, grinning widely as he sat back and picked up his coffee cup. "My wife has fallen in love with this town and wants to stay here too."

Chloe rubbed her temples with the tips of her fingers. "Oh, this is a lot to take in."

Byron picked up his cup and sipped. "You have all the time you need to decide. I know you're getting married tomorrow, so if you…"

"I'll do it." She let out a breath, turning to Jason. "You'll be here with me?"

"As promised."

"You'll all help me finance this? I mean I have savings, but…"

Jason pulled in her in close, taking in the scent of her hair, the feel of her against him, the smile she'd flashed as she took the offer. "The world is yours, Ms. Richardson. The firm is what it is because of you. It should be yours, and I can't wait to be your partner."

CHAPTER 33

*I*n Aubrey Heights, there was a magic that buzzed on Christmas Day. The snow shimmered a bit more, the air was crisper, and Chloe Richardson woke in her childhood bed with the same excitement she'd once felt knowing Santa had come and left her the very best toys under the tree. Only this morning, that excitement was for Jason—and the vows they were about to share.

She'd decided to be a little traditional and stay at her parents' house the night before the wedding. With the Inn full of guests, Jason's mother had opted to stay with him and give her room to Byron Mason, who had accepted their invitation to stay for the wedding.

Chloe climbed from bed and moved swiftly to the window. She noticed the shimmer from the snow, and then realized just how much snow there was.

At least two more feet of snow had fallen since she'd rested her head on the pillow.

When her bedroom door opened, her mother stood there. Her hair in hot rollers, and her hand pressed to her chest. "I don't know how we're going to get to town. The roads are all closed."

"This can't be happening," Chloe turned back to the window. "Not on my wedding day."

Her mother moved in behind her and wrapped her arm around Chloe's shoulders. "Dad's trying to figure something out. Everyone else is in one location. So even if we're late, they're all there."

It made sense, she decided. She took a long, deep breath and tried to calm her nerves. She would still be married to the man she loved on Christmas, perhaps it just wouldn't be at noon.

JASON STOOD on the front porch of the Inn with Byron Mason on one side of him and Tyler Ashby on the other. In all of his life, he'd never seen so much snow.

Byron rested his hand on Jason's shoulder. "It's Christmas Day. Miracles of all sorts happen today."

Jason nodded slowly, just not sure he believed it.

"She'll be here," Tyler offered his perspective as he sipped his coffee. "She wants to marry you more than anything."

"I hope so," Jason replied and both men laughed.

Byron shoved his hands into the pockets of his coat. "She's smitten, and she has been since she met you."

Jason looked at the older man to his left. "And that's why I have a scar over my eye."

"Ah, that just built character."

Jason chuckled. Had it not been for that stapler, they'd never have had that time together to get to know one another. When he thought about it, he'd been smitten too, right from the start.

Now, he was going to marry the woman of his dreams, the one he stole a job from, and yet, Mother Nature was taking charge.

He was dressed and ready to get married, but his bride was nowhere to be seen.

Gwendolyn and Gloria walked out onto the porch and joined them. They all stood silently, bundled in their winter coats, dressed in suits and dresses beneath.

Gwendolyn took Tyler's arm. "No sign of them?"

He shook his head. "Not yet. But no one is in any hurry. They'll get married when they can get the roads open."

Jason agreed with a nod, but in his heart, he didn't believe what Tyler had said. He was in a hurry. He wanted to get married and start the new adventure of his life with Chloe. It was meant to be, and he wanted it now.

"Listen," Gloria said as she walked toward the steps of the Inn. "I hear sleigh bells. Dear Lord. Do I hear Santa?"

The rest of them followed her down the shoveled steps and shoveled walk to the street. A warmth that Jason had never known, filled him, and he thought perhaps his heart would burst.

Coming down the street, in a sleigh drawn by reindeer, was in fact Santa, with Jason's bride-to-be seated next to him. Behind them, a large snowplow with her entire family piled into the cab of the truck.

Jason moved past the rest of the group, and stood in the snowbank, as the sleigh came to a stop in front of the Inn.

"You sure know how to make an entrance, don't you?" Laughter filled his voice as he looked up at his bride, wrapped in quilts and scarves, her wedding dress peeking through. Her cheeks were a bright pink, but her smile could have melted all the snow in Aubrey Heights.

"Ho-ho-ho," Santa bellowed. "Here is your bride, son. You must have been a very good boy this year."

"I don't know about that, Santa. I think I'm just a very lucky boy."

He took Chloe's hand and helped her down from the sleigh, and right into his waiting arms.

She kissed him with cold lips. "I didn't want to wait this out. I wanted to marry you. I want to be with you forever, starting right now."

"And that is exactly what I wished for this Christmas," he promised as he scooped her up in his arms and carried her up the stairs, and into the Inn.

* * *

THE SITTING room was draped in white, with chairs of all kinds lined in little rows. Flowers had been brought from the flower shop and arranged in beautiful sprays. Melanie had found some unique crystal glasses in her store for the bride and groom to celebrate from.

Jason stood at the front of the room, Tyler standing in as his best man. The woman staying in room 210 played the Bridal March on the old—and out of tune—upright piano, and Jason watched as his beautiful bride descended the stairs with her father.

At that moment Jason wasn't sure he could remember his own name. His entire mind had turned to mush when he saw Chloe walk toward him.

Out of the corner of his eye, he saw her mother hand his mother a tissue. Yes, this was absolutely the most perfect venue and time to marry the woman of his dreams.

The man who owned the Inn stood next to him, a Bible in his hand, ready to officiate the wedding.

When she and her father reached Jason, the music

stopped. Her father kissed Chloe on the cheek, and then shook Jason's hand before sitting next to his wife.

"You're stunning," he said to Chloe, whose cheeks were now only pink because she was smiling so widely.

"And as always, you're very handsome."

"From this moment on," he promised.

"Forever and ever," she agreed as they turned to the man with the Bible and promised themselves to one another for eternity.

EPILOGUE

Chloe looked out of her office window and took in the sight of the fresh snow. She dangled the *Tiffany* bracelet in front of her, enjoying the thoughtful gift her husband had given her when they landed their newest client.

The sound of bells from a corner Santa brought a smile to her face, and she thought of her magical ride on his sleigh. What a wonderful day that had been.

Her attention was drawn back to her work when there was a tapping at her door. Standing there in a grey suit that accentuated those stunning blue eyes, stood her husband leaning against the doorjamb.

"You don't look like you're getting much done," he offered with a grin.

"I can't think straight after Thanksgiving. You know that."

"Oh, I know," he teased as he walked into her office and closed the door behind him.

They'd been married now for two years, and he was a quick study of her favorite things, she thought as he rounded her desk and sat down on it right in front of her.

"Give me your feet."

Chloe laughed a hearty laugh as she tried to hoist a foot in his direction.

Jason pulled off her slipper and began to massage. "You should have stayed home," he said as he rubbed her aching arch.

"There's too much to do. Tyler just sent me the contracts back for his new chain of coffee houses, and Gloria…"

"Can all wait until after the new year. You're in no condition to be working."

Chloe let out a grunt and placed her hands on her enormous belly. "Mom says the house is all decorated in Aubrey Heights."

"I know. She called me to see what time we would be arriving."

"Do you think we really should go? I mean, look at me." She rested her hand on her stomach as the two babies inside fought for space.

"I've never seen you look more beautiful. The roads are fine, and if we leave here right after work, we'll be safe. Then you will be forced to take it easy."

Chloe set her foot on the ground and gave Jason her hands so he could help pull her from the chair. "Thank you."

"You're welcome." He cupped her face in his hands.

"I mean for agreeing to go back to Aubrey Heights to have the babies, and to stay longer than planned."

Jason chuckled. "Thank you for agreeing to let my mom stay with us while we are there."

"I wouldn't have wanted it any other way. I can't wait for the babies to see their bedrooms in their house, surrounded by the quaint sounds of Christmas, and then the one here in the city. You certainly did give me the best of everything."

"You deserve it. There is nothing I wouldn't do for

the woman who loves me unconditionally and has gone through all of this to give me two more little girls to love."

"I know they will love you as much as I do."

"Then I most certainly am the luckiest man in the world."

Chloe wrapped her arms around Jason's neck and kissed him gently, then she ran her finger over the faint scar above his eyebrow. "You just never know how things are going to turn out, do you?"

Jason lifted her chin with his finger and directed her gaze back to him. "Oh, I knew. I knew when I took that job that it would be a corporate Christmas present, and my life would change forever."

MEET THE AUTHOR

Bestselling Author Bernadette Marie is known for building families readers want to be part of. Her series *The Keller Family* has graced bestseller charts since its release in 2011. Since then she has authored and published over thirty-five books. The married mother of five sons promises romances with a *Happily Ever After always...* and says she can write it because she lives it.

Obsessed with writing since the age of 12, Bernadette Marie officially started her journey as an author in 2007 when she finalized a manuscript she'd been writing for 22 years, shelved it, and wrote 12 more books that year. In 2009 she was contracted with a small publisher in a deal that would eventually go bad. From that experience, she knew she could take control of her career and that's what she did.

A chronic entrepreneur since opening her first salon at the age of twenty, Bernadette Marie established her own publishing house in 2011, *5 Prince Publishing,* so that she could publish the books she liked to write and help make the dreams of other aspiring authors come true too. Believing there is a place for the fresh author's voice, she not only publishes but coaches others who wish to publish their work independently.

Bernadette Marie is the happily married mother of five hockey playing boys. When she is not in the stands, she and her husband run their family business together. She is a lover of stout craft beers and has an addiction to all things chocolate.

www.ingramcontent.com/pod-product-compliance
Lightning Source LLC
Chambersburg PA
CBHW030524020726
47494CB00004B/1225